10TH ANNI

VIGILANTES
of love

JOHN EVERSON

VIGILANTES
of love

21 tales of the dark and light

JOHN EVERSON

DARKARTS

B O O K S

NAPERVILLE, ILLINOIS

~2013~

Dedication

For Geri, who taught me
about fighting for love.

Acknowledgments

Many of these stories would never have seen print but for
the encouragement of some very special editors, and I want
to thank Marybeth O'Halloran, Pat Nielsen, Shane Ryan
Staley, Dave Barnett, Tina Jens and many more for their
critiques and encouragement over the years.
Whatever seeds I planted, they helped grow.
I've been richer for the nurturing.

VIGILANTES OF LOVE

Printed in the United States of America.
First Dark Arts Books Printing, April 2013
ISBN-13: 978-0615-80860-4
ISBN-10: 0-615-80860-3

B O O K S

TABLE OF CONTENTS

Only in the darkness, can you see the stars...

—*Martin Luther King, Jr.*

10th Anniversary Edition
of *Vigilantes of Love*

T his year, 2013, marks the 20th anniversary of my career as an author of dark fiction.

Oh, sure, I wrote stories prior to 1993... I wrote short stories all the way back in grade school, and published one in my high school newspaper, actually. But it was in 1993 that I began sending out my stories to national magazines, and it was in the spring of that year that I received my first acceptances for "Learning to Build" and "Preserve," both of which appear in this collection.

2013 also marks the 10th anniversary of the release of *Vigilantes of Love*, my second book-length collection, first published by Chicago's Twilight Tales (which, sadly, has not survived to issue this 10th anniversary edition, hence its new home with Dark Arts Books).

I had written and published dozens of short stories in the 1990s, but never connected during that period with the local community of writers and genre readers. I wrote my stories on weekends, and dropped them in the mail to magazines and crossed my fingers that they'd find a home. And that was that. Other than some e-mails via AOL, I didn't "talk shop" with other writers, or participate in critique groups.

But when my first book-length collection, *Cage of Bones & Other Deadly Obsessions*, was published in 2000, I began reaching out to connect with the local horror writer/reader community. I discovered a group in Chicago called Twilight Tales, which hosted live fiction readings every Monday night in a purportedly haunted bar in Chicago (The Red

Lion, which has since been razed). I found I really enjoyed performing the fiction, as well as meeting other writers of the "dark side," and for a few years, spent as many Monday nights in Chicago as I could (not always an easy feat, since I lived out in the far west suburbs!)

In addition to hosting a live reading series, Twilight Tales published occasional anthologies. In 2002, I sold them a trio of stories for an anthology called *Freaks, Geeks & Sideshow Floozies*, and, since my dayjob involved desktop publishing, I ended up getting involved on the technical side to help with the layout of the cover artwork. Later in the year, when the group decided they were going to branch out from just doing chapbooks and occasional anthologies to publish single-author collections, I threw my hat in the ring to be considered for one. *Cage of Bones* had pulled together my best "hardcore" horror work published in various magazines in the '90s. But it ignored the other side of my writing. While I wrote a lot of erotic horror, I had also written a lot of stuff that was lighter in tone. And I loved those stories just as much.

Tina Jens, the founder of Twilight Tales (and editor of the book line) was receptive to the idea, and so was born *Vigilantes of Love*, almost the antithesis of my first collection. Originally, the collection was going to focus on stories with a music theme inherent in the fantasy. I didn't end up having enough material to make that pan out, but you will find stories like "Lovesong" and "A Time For Music" here due to that initial theme.

The book was actually titled "Vigilantes of Love" before there was a story of the same name. I just liked the sound of that title, and it was sort of a musical nod at New Order.

We were on deadline, doing final edits to the collection via e-mail the weekend before it went to press, when I came up with the idea of a story *called* "Vigilantes of Love" that explored a zombie curse connected to lust and the full moon. I wrote that short tale one night and Tina liked it, but pushed me to expand it to be more of a full tale, rather than just a vignette. I didn't know at the time if I could flesh it out in such a short span of time, but by the end of Sunday night, I had it. We dropped it in at the end of the book and the result is what you read here. Ironically, several people since then have told me the story should be expanded more, into a novel. I've outlined an idea for one, but have not, so far, had the opportunity to write it. Maybe by 2023!

Before *Vigilantes* was actually in production, I had taken over handling the layout and cover artwork of Twilight Tales' bookline. And that's how I found myself in the unanticipated position in 2003 of creating the cover art for my second book. That probably doesn't seem strange now, actually, in an era when everyone is publishing their own work on the fly, but a decade ago, most authors felt that the legitimate route to publishing was to sell your work to a publisher who would a) pay you, and b) take care of all that layout/artwork/editing sort of stuff on their own. I stumbled into a hybrid of that, since I sold my second book to a publisher just as I was also taking on some of that publisher's design and layout work.

In the end... *Vigilantes of Love* turned out to be not only my second book-length collection, but also my first full-fledged collage graphic cover. I had helped Twilight Tales out with graphic tweaks to a couple of other covers previously, but my work there was basically augmenting the illustrative art created by other artists. With *Vigilantes* and in short order, John Weagly's *Undertow of Small Town Dreams*, I created my first start-to-finish photo collage covers... and I found I really loved working in that medium. Since then, I've ended up doing covers for Twilight Tales, Delirium Books, Bad Moon Books and my own Dark Arts Books. Two dozen published book covers, in all!

A very unexpected side-career.

I think my design skills have improved a little over the years, and so for this 10th anniversary edition of *Vigilantes of*

Love, I have revisited the cover. I didn't want to completely dispense with the original, but it was always just a little too busy, without a focal point, and with a title font that didn't read very well when reduced to a thumbnail. So I went back to the original art elements, moved some things around and added in a new photo to give the montage some balance, and a focal point (thanks to my cover art model and wife, Geri, who now provides a center to this cover, as she does to the rest of my life!) I also changed the titling so you can actually read it better when it's reduced to thumbnails on the Internet or smartphones. The original artwork piece, sans titling, appears on the title page inside the book.

There were several stories that were considered for the original edition of *Vigilantes of Love* that we decided to drop at the time, in order to keep the book to a "thin" paperback. I've opted to add some of those that have never been collected in my other books as "Bonus Stories" to this anniversary edition.

A lot has happened over the past 10 years. When this book first was released, I still had yet to publish a novel. I've since published six, with a seventh on the way. When this book was first released, there were no Kindles or Nooks or iPads. The era of indie "print" publishing was in its short-lived prime.

There have been a lot of changes in the world since 2003.

I think, however, that the stories within, remain relevant. The emotion of the human heart does not change with technology.

We will always be driven to do what we do with our lives by love. For better... or worse.

— John Everson
Naperville, IL
January, 2013

INTRODUCTION:

The Songs of Love

L ove is a funny thing. It can make life worth living, and it can make life a living hell. Poets and songwriters have opined on its dichotomies for centuries, but that hasn't changed the essential warring nature of human emotion. Driven by love, we will alternately lie, cheat, kill, kiss, caress and serve. It's an insubstantial thing, this emotion, and yet its power rivals religions, kings and common sense.

The stories in this volume explore some of the strange intersections of love, from the bent bonds of the parent-child relationship to the stirrings of first amour and the bittersweet torture of adult love tasted and tempered by time and lust.

Love is like fire — it can warm you when you're cold, protect you when you're alone, and burn you if it rages out of control.

Love is also like a song. And many of these stories revolve around music, from a child's faery flute to a piano carved out of a most unusual substance. Music has amazing powers: it can catch and seduce a lover, as well as heal a broken heart after that lover is gone.

These stories are all love songs — to a genre of music and a gone-but-not-forgotten favorite record store, to cities special to the heart, and to the lover's best friend; the moon.

I hope you'll revel in these stories and celebrate the many faces of love... even when the love turns evil.

— Tina L. Jens
Chicago, IL
March 2003

Calling of the Moon

Six months have gone since Eva passed on. And still I wrestle with the memories she left me. I fear those nights, the cool fingers of moonlight creeping like airy feelers across the sill, the Oriental wall hanging, the carpet.

Before you say what I know you're thinking, let me tell you — my remembrances of Eva were not memories of silken touches beneath the hidden folds of white tablecloths or amid the cool cotton sheets of her bed. Eva was not a lover to me, though now I sleep in her bed. But I loved her just the same. She saved my life because of her sight... but I was too blind to save hers.

Have you ever watched an accident and known, seconds before the splintering, shattering crash of impact, that one car is aimed inexorably at disaster? "That guy's going to hit him," you say to yourself, and then, pow, slam, scream, he does. That must be how Eva saw me.

Oh, it was nothing so dramatic as a car careening into a wall or a man perched to jump from a ledge. I wasn't waiting to throw my body upon the algaed rocks of the ocean when she came along and swept me back to my senses. And yet, that's exactly what happened.

Sure, I was on the street, but it could have been months, or years — or never — before I got the courage to finally jump from the edge to become waterlogged fishbait in the bay.

"You need to open your eyes," she said the first time we met. In fact, I think it was the first thing Eva ever said to me.

At the time, my eyes were blurry slits wishing away the light, but even so I could see that hers were dark pools of brown, her hair a shelf of granite, slight curls like the chiseled locks of a Grecian statue. She was a solid woman, and an intense one. If cover girls commanded attention with the set of their proud breasts and dripping gloss lips, Eva commanded at least as much attention with the hawkish fierceness of her gaze, the whiplash shock of her tongue. I was drunk the first time she spoke to me, and still drunk the last.

I haven't touched a bottle since.

"Yeah, and what is there to see if I did?" I mumbled back at her, a cesspool of pity and pathos. I could have been the poster child for "poor me."

"Open them and find out," she insisted.

I shooed her with a flopping hand. "Time enough for that tomorrow. When it's light out."

"You strike me as the sort of man who might see most clearly by the light of the moon," she said. "But suit yourself."

And with that, she walked away, blue and white checked housecoat swishing at her thick white ankles. I noted the attitude of that walk blurrily, then turned my limited attention back to the sidewalk.

There were some fascinating crack patterns near the bricks of the bar behind me, and some ants that evidently couldn't quite dig their way to China, but had at least come up from beneath the earth near Chinatown. I curled into a ball and kissed the earth they walked upon.

I didn't aspire to much in those days. King of ants and street lice I was, and proud of it. Well, maybe not proud — the hours sucked and the clothes stunk — but certainly not too put-out about the situation. I didn't care. Not about the old lady with the heavy brown eyes, not about the stink on my mud-stained grey trousers, and not about the blur in my vision.

"G'night ant," I slurred at the creeping black creature near my face, then prepared to join him in the land of the undead. *I hope his cousin is still ferrying souls to the right side of the river,* I thought and then I was asleep in the comforting arms of the sidewalk.

Life was a simple downward slide.

* * * * *

"Just knock when it's morning, I'll open the door."

That's what Eva promised the first morning I was due to deliver her coffee.

That was her fee. I brought her a super grande Starbucks (a buck eighty at the time) and she gave me three dollars. Not a major income for one day, but shit, it bought a burger without the need to panhandle for two or three hours. The thing of it was, she never paid me up front — smart on her part. So those first few days, it was like I had no job. I had to hold onto my dollar commission to buy her coffee the next day just so I could make another buck the next morning. But it worked out. She tossed me a five on one of those first days and ended up making ten bucks that first week. So I came back.

Every morning at 8 a.m. I delivered a Starbucks to her door.

"I'm too old to be hiking down the block at that hour," she told me. "You're already there. So you get me my coffee and I'll pay ya."

She kept her word, and I kept mine. Pretty soon, she devised some other projects that pulled me off the street during the afternoons. She had one of those top-of-Nob Hill houses with an old-fashioned charm. Which, to most folk, simply means big upkeep. And it did. That house needed painting and caulking and new window screens and trim... I did it all for her that summer, 'til the house looked just like all the other tall thin reach-for-the-sky gables. Complete with garish pink paint. I tried to talk her out of that, but she wasn't a lady to listen when she'd made up her mind.

"See that green house over there?" she pointed when I complained about the paint she'd picked. I grimaced.

19

"Well, I'm not asking you to paint it green now, am I?" she said, as if that simple fact made garish pink alright.

I didn't care much, though — she gave me fifty bucks for the paint which I knew I could get for under twenty, so who was I to argue? It wasn't my house. Best thing about it was, while thirty dollars of profit might not seem a lot to people who make that in an hour, I knew that so long as I was working on Eva's place, she'd be bringing out sandwiches and snacks and a can of Coke now and then. So that was thirty bucks free and clear. And on top of that, she gave me ten dollars a day for the labor.

I spent a lot of time at Eva's place. Every now and then, she'd call me into the house, sit me down at the honey pine table she used in her kitchen.

"How are you seeing these days?" she asked me one time, just after I'd finished giving her old Chevy a tuneup. Don't know why she had me do it since I'd never seen it out of the garage — thought I'd choke to death on the blue smoke the first time I got it turned over.

"Ma'am?" I asked.

"Cracks in the sidewalk and stink in your nose aren't the only bit of life open to you's what I mean."

Eva wasn't nothing if not blunt.

I nodded. Taking a soaring double somersault leap off the Bay Bridge wasn't seeming quite as seductive since the day Eva had walked by my private slab of public concrete.

She was an odd one. Some of her stories were crazier than the tales of fame, fortune and bent-over babes that I'd heard about for months out on the street from cross-eyed bottom feeders who you could track by smell for three blocks. They claimed to have been to the big time and back, but I knew better. The big time wouldn't leave you high and dry like we were. No angel had ever fallen this far, not even the black one.

I loved to listen to Eva talk. About growing up in a small English castle out in the country or of how she chased a man all the way to Israel before abruptly chalking him up as a fool's errand and instead joining a kibbutz. Was it all real? I don't know. It sounded as flaky as any street talk, but for some reason, I believed her. She had a son shuffling papers somewhere in Africa for a blue chip and a daughter whose occasional letters from Des Moines were always covered in smiley face stickers and smelled faintly of soapy perfume. I knew because one of my duties quickly became picking her mail up at the post office.

While her life, in story, seemed a grand adventure and her sometimes hard-to-swallow retellings profoundly rational, I had to admit that she had a deep-end thing going on about the moon. She first explained it to me over a lunch of peanut butter and cherry jelly, while I was on a break from painting the shutters. Pink. Geez.

"It's coming 'round again tonight, I can feel it," she proclaimed while I was in the midst of tonguing the chunky glue off my palate. For a moment, I thought she meant her period, which had to be a memory two decades past, at least. But Eva would talk about anything, so I wasn't too surprised.

"I can never sleep when it does," she said, her voice growing far away, dreamy. Her face relaxed then, and as the lines smoothed away, I caught a glimpse of the girl she'd once been.

It's so hard to look at old people as anything other than old, but I guessed that Eva had once been a beautiful woman. The kind who trails allure like incense. I could imagine a line of men chasing her as she followed her faux Romeo to the land of the Bible.

I didn't know what to say, so I played the employee. "Ma'am?" I said, once I unstuck the roof of my mouth.

"The moon," she answered while reaching over to wipe a dollop of cherry jelly from my face with a cloth napkin.

"I can feel its pull when the moon is full. Always have. When I was a girl, my mother used to wake in the middle of the night and find me wandering in the topiary during the nights of the full moon. I never remembered how I got there. The doctor just said I was sleepwalking, but my mother soon realized that my walking episodes coincided with the phase of the moon. She would padlock the outside of my door once a month to keep me inside."

She looked at me searchingly then and said, "Most people are too wound up in their lives to listen, but you've been out on the street during the full moon. Have you ever felt its tug?"

I shook my head no and she sighed, disappointed. "It gets stronger for me every year. It probably sounds crazy to you, but after all, they named lunatics after Luna, yes?"

I laughed along with her quiet chuckle, not knowing what else to say. She did sound a bit off.

"Sometimes, as a young woman, when I did sleep during the night of the moon, I would feel my soul pull away from my body and drift upwards, outwards, towards the window where the silvery light was reaching inside. I would look down at my own sleeping face and wonder, just for a second, who that was sleeping in my bed. And then the shock of who I was seeing, that realization would hit me and I'd panic, reaching out for my body and I would fall, inward, and wake up gasping for air."

She paused then, a crooked smile on her face. "A couple experiences like that and I began to close my shutters each month. I wondered where the moon would take me, but I wasn't ready to go just yet."

It was several weeks later when I first felt that pull myself. Maybe it was the power of suggestion and my strong imagination working in tandem, but I know I felt something.

I was walking late along the water near the Embarcadero, and the lights of the Bay gleamed blurrily through the fog rolling in. The red warning lights blinked for aviators like angry fireflies and a snow-white cloud snaked around the metal struts below. The omnipresent San Francisco fire engines blared fuzzily in the distance, and above me, I felt the cool white hand of the moon on my back.

She was gentle but firm. It was as if, for a second, both my feet left the ground and I was propelled forward. My arms pinwheeled to restore my balance.

Two steps farther forward and I'd have been swimming.

I jerked around to see who had pushed me. There was only empty sidewalk.

I started to jog, telling myself it was nothing, and a little exercise would get my blood flowing. I'd just been falling asleep on my feet. But my jog turned into a run which took me all the way to the dollar-a-night hotel I was calling home just off Taylor Street.

In moments I'd left the cool creamy gleam of the moon on the bay behind for the echoes and fog of the inner city.

The next morning, I was at Eva's place extra early, waiting for those gaudy pink shutters to open. On any other day of the month, I could have yelled through an open screen. She loved to feel the air slide across her at night, she said. Her windows were almost never closed in the spring, summer and fall. But last night belonged to the moon, and Eva hid from her hand. The hand that I now believed I had felt.

"I hope it's hot," she demanded, when she finally opened the door to my knocking, still in her long faded floral nightgown. She passed the back of her hand across her eyes and rubbed. "I barely caught a wink last night, but I don't intend to waste the day abed."

She pushed the screen door open and motioned me inside. "Come in, come in. Sometimes you're slower than my auntie Jane's molasses."

I set the coffee on the kitchen table and turned to leave.

"What's the matter?" she asked, holding my shoulder. "You don't feel right."

"Just a dream," I shrugged and grabbed for the latch.

"Sit down, boy," she insisted, and dragged me over to the kitchen table.

"It's nothing, Eva, really. An overactive imagination is all."

Her eyes bored into me and accepted no excuses. So I told her my story of walking by the bay in the moonlight. And of feeling the moon trying to push me in.

She nodded knowingly, then grinned. "I knew you could hear her, if you only listened," she said. As if this were a good thing. "Now you won't think I'm a crazy for drawing my shutters."

I didn't say anything. She took my hands in her own. "I've been telling her no for so long, sometimes I wonder myself why. I've spent these past weeks enjoying your company, but sooner or later, I have to answer her. She may have pushed your shoulder, but it's my attention she's trying to get."

I didn't say anything as she sipped a loud slurp of coffee through the plastic spout.

"You stay in on the night of the full moon from now on, you hear?"

I agreed. Then she turned the conversation to her daughter in Des Moines. Eventually she shooed me out to my painting, as if I had been the one insisting on dawdling at her table.

* * * * *

Not long after that, I bought myself a secondhand pair of Dockers and a button-down pale blue shirt that didn't have five or six stains down the middle, and got myself a part-time job at the Chinese grocery down on Hyde.

They didn't say anything about my coming to work in the same clothes every day since I was careful to wash out my shirt every night in the sink. I used my first paycheck to buy three more outfits.

Two more paychecks and I moved into a tiny studio apartment. It was south of Market, but I was off the street and out of the tuberculosis hotels. I hung my meager ward-robe in the single closet off the kitchen, with hangers from Eva, and scrubbed the floors clean of grease and mold with wire mesh and a towel I found in a dumpster out back. There wasn't much to boast about in the place — it had no air conditioning (a noticeable detraction as the heat began to rise and the fog disappear), no bed (I slept on the floor on a rolled-up pair of jeans) and the kitchen was really just a sink and a half-sized refrigerator sitting on scuffed tan tile in the corner of the room. The refrigerator rattled danger-ously whenever the cooling element kicked on.

But it was mine.

And while the lock was less secure than the two rusted hinges on the front door, I didn't have anything I was wor-ried about the street boys stealing. It was hard to believe, but life was actually looking up.

It was a Wednesday afternoon, weeks later, when I fi-nally finished all the painting on her house and garage that Eva could possibly devise. The air was scented with salt and longing. Long rays of sunshine colored the ground in tints of amber and yellow, and the roses on Eva's porch smelled stronger than bottled musk.

The day before, a girl who I'd seen before eyeing me along with the lettuce heads at the grocery finally braved the fates to talk to me.

"Where is the soy sauce?" she asked, admittedly not a personal question, but I took it as a good sign. She was Chi-nese and had shopped there as long as I'd worked there. She knew where the soy sauce was.

I vaulted up the steps to Eva's door filled with the sauce of a man on the rise. My brushes were clean, there was five dollars in my pocket and there was a pretty black-haired girl who might be stopping by the grocery tonight because she'd "forgotten" an item yesterday. My world was blue and green and bright.

But Eva's face was otherwise.

25

"Can you drive?" she asked me when I got to the door.

"Well, I don't have a license anymore, but sure, I used to drive," I said.

"Take me to the airport."

Eva bade me stay at her place until she came home from her daughter's in Des Moines, so she could phone me to say when she'd be back and I could pick her up at the airport. I couldn't afford a phone at my apartment.

What was supposed to be a few days of absence stretched longer when her daughter didn't pull through. She was gone for weeks; after the death and funeral, she called to say she was hopping another plane to stay for a while with her son in Africa. It was Eva all the way. I shook my head and smiled at the thought of this little old spitfire touching down on the Ivory Coast.

At 8:13 a.m. on a Saturday (her stove had one of those electric digital clocks) as I sat reading her paper at her table in her kitchen, after a night on her couch (I wouldn't sleep in her bed — it just didn't seem right) the phone call finally came.

"Pick me up at three this afternoon," she said. "At the United terminal. I'm ready to come home."

I almost didn't recognize her when she came out of the terminal, lugging the one canvass bag she'd packed before leaving, along with two new plastic bags lumpy with additions. You don't ever come back with less than you take. Always more.

Eva had also come back with more on her mind. She'd aged two decades in two months. Suddenly she seemed as frail and weathered as an oak leaf in December. I didn't know what to say to her. When she'd left it was to help her daughter after a car accident, and she'd come back without any daughter at all.

I pushed her bags into the trunk and got the door for her, but she insisted on closing it herself.

"Get in the car," she said, shooing me away from the handle. "Let's just get home."

It was a long, quiet ride from the airport; Eva stared out the window at the bay, and I tried not to punch the unfamiliar brakes too hard. I'd owned a car once but that had been many years before. Eva's Chevy probably predated my Honda, but I hadn't driven it while she was gone.

When we got home, I picked up the couple of items I'd brought with me from home — a recently acquired toothbrush and my laundry — and headed for the door, eager to leave her with her own thoughts. "I'm sorry," I mumbled, staring at the floor of her kitchen and clumsily shifting my plastic sack of belongings from one hand to the other.

Eva nodded. "Don't forget my coffee," was all she said.

* * * * *

By the end of October she seemed back to normal. Mostly. I only really saw her in the mornings, bringing her that one-cup care package that had managed to pull me off the street and into a full-time job at the grocery store (the stockboy had quit a couple weeks before) and a one-room apartment on the skid. The week before I'd even asked the Chinese girl, Soo Lee, to a movie.

And she said yes.

"Have you heard from the moon lately?" Eva asked me one morning.

I shook my head no.

"Not since that night," I replied. "I took your advice; I stay in when the moon is full."

Actually, I had long ago begun to think the incident was a product of a mind ripe with street delirium.

She nodded absently. "Just as well. There are still things here for you to do."

I looked around at the freshly varnished cupboards, the recently painted back door, the newly screened front windows and put my hands out in askance.

"What?"

She smiled sadly and shook her head. "Tell me about your little Chinese girl. Will you take her out again?"

In fact, I did take her out again. And again. And two weeks later, I introduced her to Eva.

"This is Soo Lee," I said, beaming with pride. Slurring with pride too; we'd just come from Happy Hour.

"Would you like some tea?" Eva invited, but I declined.

"We're off to Perrone's for dinner."

Perrone's was just a diner, but for me it was living high. As Soo Lee stepped down from the porch, Eva pressed a ten dollar bill into my hand.

"Get her whatever she wants," she said. "And you… stay off the wine tonight."

I knew better than to argue.

That night, as I walked Soo Lee home by the light of the moon, I felt a touch on my shoulders once again. This time though, it wasn't a push, but a cool caress along my neck and shoulder blades.

At first I thought it was Soo Lee's fingers running down my back, but then I realized her hand was in mine. I shivered in the night breeze. She smiled at me, her eyes dark with compassion. "You are chilled?"

"No," I said, glancing behind me. "Your hand keeps me warm."

She kissed me on the cheek and it was so.

The next morning, the hill to Eva's house seemed flat as Ohio. I was as jaunty as a boy after his first date, and I longed to share my story with Eva, the woman who'd made it all possible.

I was early with her coffee, but I couldn't wait. Her shutters were already open as I vaulted up the steps and called inside.

"Eva? Coffee Boy."

I'd called myself Coffee Boy since the first week of bringing her this morning treat, though I looked farther from a boy every day.

There was no answer.

I tried the latch. The door was open, so I stepped inside. I set the coffee down on the table, saw a paper with my name on it. I unfolded it and read the cramped, tiny script addressed to me.

It was the first note I had received in years. And the worst ever.

> *Drink the coffee, Antonio. It's yours. Tonight I will sleep with the shutters undone. She has called me for too long. I must answer.*
>
> *My daughter is gone before me, my son is a world away. And you... you are my finest child. But you do not need me any longer. Already I can feel her pulling me to the windows, and it is only eight o'clock. She barely wakes.*
>
> *Drink the coffee, Antonio. And bring your bride to live in my home. You'll find, in my will, that it is yours now. Aren't you glad you painted it pink? Now you may repaint it blue if you like! Or purple! I have only one request: close the shutters on the night of the moon and hold your Soo Lee tight then. The moon has called you once, and she will never forget you. Nor will I.*
>
> *— Eva*

"Eva?" I called again, but it came out as a whispered croak.

The morning light was climbing with heavy orange fingers through the front room, and sliding down the walls in her bedroom. I didn't have to move much to look across the hallway and see that her bed was still made, and the white stockinged foot atop it lay still and silent.

I couldn't go into her room then. Instead, I sat down at her table, and slowly, with tremulous slurps, drank her coffee.

Lovesong

"I've seen a lot of broken hearts in time
and I've had my share as well
Every story's different
but the pain's the same, they tell."

– *Industrial Disease, "Why Fall In Love?"*

She worked at the Record Stop and her name was Lissa. I write this down because they're both gone now. Something should remain, even if it's only the fragment of my memory. Call this my love story to Lissa. And the Stop. I do miss them both. Maybe you do, too.

Of course, the first time I tried to get her attention, I was looking at her name badge sideways and I got it wrong. I called out "Hey Lisa," and her manager cranked his head sideways and gave me a "you moron" look. But he didn't say anything. They called him "The Master," which was also the name of the alternative radio show he did late night on the local public radio station.

"It's Lissa," she corrected softly, drawing out the "S" as a smile lit up that wan, thin face. She had dark wide eyes shadowing a face barely wide enough to encircle them. Her chin was narrow and her hair an intricate black maze of braids and colored beads. I think I loved her the first time I saw her. I like to think she was sweet on me, too, even if I got her name wrong.

"Can I help you?" she asked, and I suddenly realized that I had absolutely nothing in mind to ask her. One of the store's cats darted between my legs and I followed its path with my eyes, looking for something to pin a question on.

"Um, yeah," I said. My eyes settled on a poster for Mabel's, the black-painted rock bar across the street. "Do you have the new Savage Republic in yet?"

She followed my gaze to the concert poster. Savage Republic was scheduled to play on Friday.

"Yeah, I think so," she said. "Over here."

She slipped out from behind the cluttered counter and led me through the stacks of just-bought and unfiled used records to the "What's New" display in the center of the store. I followed, watching the paramecia of her purple and black paisley skirt swish and swim as she moved. When she pointed to the album, displayed amid a jumble of other unfamiliar titles, I barely even looked at it, just grabbed it with one hand. I couldn't take my eyes off her.

She didn't seem to notice, though. She pursed her lips in a quick smile and continued down the aisle.

"Thanks," I called after her, holding the album in my hands. I didn't really want it; I had never heard of Savage Republic before, and I never bought new records; didn't have the cash for such extravagance. But I spent nearly everything in my wallet to buy it that day. Turns out it was pretty cool.

The next time I was in, I remember Lissa was at the counter as I vaulted up the claustrophobic stairs from the busy street below. Record Stop was on the second floor of the campus main street, and its narrow flight of painted steps was worth exploring all by itself. Years of graffiti covered the grey walls on the climb up, promoting bands and bars and, naturally, promiscuous sorority girls. She smiled when she saw I was waiting at the edge of the counter for her attention, and pointed me in the direction of the latest new underground release from the Bomp label.

Lissa turned me on to a *lot* of cool bands over the next few weeks. Record Stop was the ultimate college music store in the '80s; its walls were covered with posters of alternative artists (back when the word "alternative" actually defined something) and were filled in equal measures with cool Europop LPs from Ultravox and Yello and Alison Moyet to the more obscure but national underground bands like Husker Du and The Mekons to local artists like The Elvis Brothers and Paul Chastain (who a decade later would find his niche backing up Matthew Sweet). R.E.M. had set the guitar world on its ear with *Murmur* a couple years before and instead of the blistering power anthem solos of the '70s, the store was usually filled with the echoey strumming of Galaxie 500 or the ethereal dark gothicism of Dead Can Dance and The Cocteau Twins. Or Romeo Void. Or Colourbox. You usually didn't know what the hell the noise was coming from the speakers, but it was always edgy. Blurred vocals for blurred moods. You felt connected to something secret and powerful when you stood still and lingered in Record Stop.

"Who's that you're playing?" I'd ask Lissa, after roaming the store a few minutes and listening to the often cacophonous sound raging through the store. I didn't want it to look like I'd come in just to see her. But I had.

"The Flaming Lips," she said once when I asked about one particularly noisy bit of treble-heavy, punky distortion. "They suck," I proclaimed.

"They're playing Chin's tomorrow," she said, pointing out the LIVE FROM NEBRASKA poster by the door.

"Think they'll hire a lead singer by then?"

She grinned. I thought maybe I had a chance with her.

"Who do *you* like?" I asked.

She tilted her head, staring at the ceiling for a moment and then slowly began to twirl around.

"Everything," she proclaimed with drama, hands reaching out towards the wall displays that featured the latest from Joy Division, Bauhaus, Psychedelic Furs, The dB's, and more. The New Releases wall was always my favorite because it had such diversity, and spotlighted all these bizarre albums that never hit the front window displays of other stores. Of course, the discs the chain record stores featured in their window displays weren't even available at the Stop. Each one of Record Stop's wall picks had a little circular sticker on it with a one or two-sentence description penned by the store manager. My favorite for weeks was an album by some band called Dali's Car that had a cover seemingly captured in heaven. The album was like a classic painting: two figures flanked by Roman pillars, all the colors washed in skyblue and gold. I never bought it, but it looked excellent — a magical moment captured and shared without permission of the divine.

"Even this?" I asked about the Flaming Lips song currently blaring.

"Sure," she said. "They have energy."

And then came my delivery. "You wanna go see them tomorrow with me?"

"You don't want to see them," she said. "But thanks."

She winked at me and slipped away down the aisle, one of the store's cats leaping across the record bins to follow her. The grey one I think.

I sneezed and the opportunity was lost. She'd started talking to another guy who was leafing through the racks of $1.99 specials.

I always sneezed in that store. I loved coming inside and browsing the racks and racks of albums, from the late '60s Simon & Garfunkel and Seals and Crofts albums reeking of the mold from someone's flooded basement, to the Ambrosia and Toto leftovers of the '70s to the black and white, obscene cartoonish covers of the underground singles from the latest local bands of the '80s. Between the mold from old water damaged records and the cats, I always left with a runny nose.

In the back of the store was a small video rental section. Classic kitsch and cult fare — *A Clockwork Orange*, Peter Seller's *Pink Panther* movies, a good selection of Russ Meyer's films (including *Faster Pussycat, Kill, Kill*, as I recall), Hammer horror films and even, I think, *I Spit On Your*

Grave. Behind that was a stairway leading up. I asked Lissa where it went to one day, and she shrugged.

"I think they keep extra stock and stuff there."

"You've never been there?"

She looked puzzled for a second, then said, "Nope," and smiled. "Not allowed."

"Not allowed?"

She shrugged again and breezed away, leaving me craning to see up the blue-grey painted steps to the dark brown wooden door at the top. The black cat slid between my legs and leapt to the third step, then turned to stare at me, green eyes flaring.

I let it go. I wish that had been the last I'd thought of it. But my mind does grab onto things and chew and chew.

Another day, as I dashed past the stairway scrawl proclaiming The Slits as the best babes ever, Lissa was alone at the counter, and I went right to her.

"Hey," I said. "Heard anything good lately?"

She was wearing a deep blue summer dress, tie-dyed with waves of purple and blue. It made her look pale, but beautiful. Her hair hung in lazy black twists over her shoulders, and her eyes seemed especially dark. I wondered if she'd been out drinking at Mabel's the night before.

"No," she said, covering a yawn with her hand.

"Catch a show last night?"

She shook her head, again.

We talked about something, just B.S., and behind me a couple of punkers came in, hair bright pink and alert like the crest of a cockatoo. The Master started towards the front of the store and Lissa whispered.

"C'mon, he's in a bad mood today."

We walked to the back of the store and he scowled at me as I went past. This was a guy you didn't want to piss off. His soft spoken descriptions of the barrage of guitar distortion that he played on his radio show were a stark contrast to the waist length black hair and steel blue eyes that seemed to pop out of his skull when he looked right at you. He was probably a nice guy, but he looked like he could rip your arm off and then laugh about it. I avoided him when I could.

Back by the cult videos, I nodded toward the stairs.

"The Master's busy, wanna see what's up there?"

I swear she trembled at the suggestion.

"No, I couldn't," she said. She clutched the doorjamb as she peered up the stairs, but then pulled herself back as if from vertigo.

"Aren't you curious what's up there?" I asked. Call me the devil.

"Yeah," she admitted slowly. "But if he catches me up there… today would be a bad day to try."

I let it go. "You busy tonight?"

"Yeah."

Strike two.

I think it was Lissa who convinced me to buy the first This Mortal Coil record, *It'll End In Tears,* because I can't play it even now without thinking of her. Not long after, I bought their second, the double album *Filigree & Shadow,* too. Back in college, I used to turn all the lights off and lie on the floor listening to the reverb-drenched tape loops and haunting voices, as if it was the music of angels. It sure sounded like it.

"You can just feel the other side," she told me. She was right.

"You can always trust an artist if they have soul," she said once.

"You mean, like, Aretha Franklin?" I asked, leery. I never liked Aretha.

"No, I mean…" she pointed at a grotesque album cover with a picture of a shrivelled, aborted baby's hand enclosed in an adult's palm. The Dead Kennedys. "Like there," she said. "They aren't afraid to put it out there. The music might be loud and abrasive, but you know they're going to go all the way. Someone who has an album cover like that is going to push to the corners of their soul for their music. Or take Cocteau Twins. You look at their albums and you know that they believe in beauty and mystery and art, and they're going to do their best to deliver it to you. They've got soul."

"So anybody who puts out an interesting album cover has soul?" I said, deliberately misinterpreting her.

She shot me a black eye.

"Noooo," she drawled. "But think of it. These bands that just pose in their tight leather pants on the cover, or even worse, hire some half naked girl to pose on their album. What does that tell you about their music? What does it say about what they think of their music? Someone who believes in their album enough to make sure the cover is beautiful or striking in some important way that relates to the music — they have soul. You can trust them to deliver something special to you."

We talked a lot about aesthetics, Lissa and I. She loved concert posters as much as album covers. You would have thought she was an art major. But she was English Lit.

"So you've got to read all that poetry crap?" I asked her once.

"Why is poetry crap but Kate Bush's lyrics are brilliant?" she countered. "Kate writes poetry. You love poetry, as long as there's a voice and a drum behind it."

I couldn't argue, so I shut up. The black cat leapt up onto the counter between us. She stroked its back and the cat arched its neck at her, turning to make sure she caressed every inch of its spine.

"Psychedelic Furs are playing Huff's Gym on Sunday," I began, but she cut me down instantly. "Poetry test on Monday," she said, and winked.

Three strikes, you're out.

I followed her to the back of the store.

The Master was off in a corner, animately discussing the merits of Throwing Muses' debut album with a pimply looking kid in a Smiths T-shirt. *Meat is Murder*, it proclaimed. "Yeah," I thought, "so is dating."

"Haven't you ever wondered what they hide up there?" I asked, back on the same obsession. I don't know what I thought was there, but I had to know. And Lissa seemed like the best way to find out. They could call the police on me, or worse, bar me from the store. But she was an employee! What would they do if they caught her, other than say, "Stay out?"

She hesitated. "I don't know."

"The Master's busy, he won't even notice," I urged. "Just take a peek."

She stepped on the first stair, and the black cat streaked ahead of her, as if to guard the way. She laughed. "See, Blackie knows I'm not supposed to go up there."

She reached down and stroked the cat's head, but it hissed at her and she drew back.

"Just go quick," I said. "He'll never know the difference. Come on, I dare ya."

She looked afraid, but then took a deep breath and hurriedly pushed herself up the stairs.

I looked back and forth from her to The Master as she climbed the steps, making sure that he didn't notice her ascent. But he didn't even glance in our direction.

I watched her from the bottom of the stairs. She was in faded jeans, a dark T-shirt and a flannel today. She was gorgeous. Delicate, but not a priss. Smart, but not a know-it-all. I had to get her to go out with me somehow.

She put her hand on the doorknob and it creaked open, throwing a slice of midday sunlight onto the dark stairwell walls.

She disappeared inside the room at the top of the stairs. She screamed.

The black cat tore past me like a bullet down the stairs and leapt onto one of the record bins. I forgot about keeping our exploration a secret. I yelled her name as I vaulted up the stairs. "Lissa?!"

It was freezing in the upper room; a window was open facing the alleyway and the faded brown drapes shifted in the March wind. There was an old wooden schoolteacher's desk in the right corner of the room and a black steel file cabinet nearby. Stacks of old LPs spilled from the room's corners.

At first I thought she'd jumped out the window, but it was only open a few inches. She couldn't have opened it, jumped and pulled it down behind her as she fell. Still, I ran to the window and looked out to see a telephone pole and empty asphalt below, a red and white Chevy Citation parked at the doorway of the red brick apartment one building over.

It was only when I turned around that I saw the blood.

Crimson and thick. Spreading.

It seemed to flow from the cracks in the floor, quickly growing from a buckets-worth to a pool.

The floor was bleeding and Lissa was gone.

"Lissa?" I called, a note of hysteria in my voice.

"Lissa?" I whispered.

The pool of blood spread out across the room, dampening the stacks of albums and staining the legs of the desk. I shivered as the late winter breeze blew in like a gale from the cracked window.

I didn't know where to turn.

"What the hell are you doing up here?"

The Master stood in the doorway, six feet of black-T-shirted, black-haired, glaring-eyed anger.

I shrunk back to the window, pointed at the floor, and babbled.

"Lissa came up here, it was my fault, I asked her to. But then she screamed and I came up and she wasn't here and there's so much blood…" which, even as I said it, I saw was untrue. The floor was only dirty brown wood. The same scuffed, turn-of-the-century narrow, dark hardwood that seemed to floor most of the buildings around the university.

The Master didn't move, only regarded me with those piercing eyes.

"Lissa hasn't been up here in a year," he said softly. "Lissa hasn't been anywhere in a year. I don't know what your deal is, kid, but I'm sick of you coming around here acting weird and talking to yourself. I think you need to get out of here. Now."

I stepped wide over the place where I'd seen the blood and left the store.

I never saw Lissa again.

But sometimes I hear her. In the guttural screams of *The Dreaming*, behind the tortured bells and echoes of *Filigree and Shadows*. It took several visits to the store for me to believe that she was gone. I tried to go when The Master was busy and ask some of the other guys working the store where she was, but they'd look puzzled or stare at me like I was crazy. "Don't know who you mean, man. No Lissa has worked here this semester," they'd say and go back to alphabetizing.

It took months until I finally learned the whole story, accidentally, during a Martial Arts class in the Phys. Ed building. The professor told it as a warning to us. Used her as a reason for us to get A's in his class. Told us of a student from the year before named Lissa. Of how she'd been putting away the day's cash in the safe one night when some asshole snuck up behind her and stabbed her in the back with a switchblade, took her money and left her to die on the bare wood floor of the upper room of the Record Stop on Main Street.

I don't know what he thought when I clenched my stomach and ran from the class.

Sometimes I feel guilty that I made her face the scene once more. As if I killed her again.

What did she see when she entered the room of her death? Did the memory of her murder come flooding back to her like a shot?

What did she think of me for sending her there?

I can still see her face some nights in the darkness when I can't sleep. I picture those taut pink lips talking of soul and honesty and expression. I see her eyes like pools of endless truth and life. Sometimes I cry, knowing the girl that I missed.

And sometimes I whisper to her. I hope she can hear. Or maybe it's better if she can't.

I want so badly to hold her tight to me, but I hope, more than anything, that my foolish curiosity set her free.

> *"But every night I lie in bed and I think of your face*
> *Remembering a better time in a gentler place*
> *All I know is that this is the hardest thing I've done*
> *and loneliness, the bitter prize I've won."*
>
> *– Industrial Disease, "Does It Have To End"*

A Time For Music

No, it *won't* feel normal again. It's all your fault anyway," Mark screamed. "You drove him away and now we'll never be a family again. I hate you!" Mark's face flared red with anger. His mother's face grew pinched and turned ghostly white. Tears glistened in both their eyes as her hand rose to slap his mouth.

Their eyes connected for one electric second and her reaction slowed.

With a mix of guilt, satisfaction and gut-bleeding emptiness, Mark turned and ran out of the kitchen and up the back stairs.

"And I hate this place!" he yelled over his shoulder, stomping heavily up the hardwood stairs.

His grandparents' house was a musty, decaying mansion tucked inconveniently away from town on a wooded hill. Mark and his mother, Marilyn Baer-Ackert — soon to be just Baer again — had moved in with them while the divorce was finalized. That meant Mark had to leave all of his friends, change schools and worst of all, live just far enough away from his new town and school that he could never go out and try to make new friends. He was a prisoner in a dying house with old, dying people. Mark felt as if he was dying himself.

He and his mother argued constantly these days. Most of the time it felt like he'd lost both of his parents.

And his grandparents weren't any help. They always sided with her, patted his shoulder and said, "She's under a lot of pressure right now, Mark, try to understand."

What about him? Did anybody ask him about the pressure he was under? No.

Did anyone ask him if he want to ride an hour every day on a bus to go to a strange school with kids who all knew each other and looked at him like some kind of alien? No.

Did anyone ask if he wanted to listen to his parents rip on each other non-stop and look to him for agreement? No.

He knew a thing or two about pressure too, but Grandma and Grandpa didn't think about that.

The grey rain beat on the window for over a half hour while Mark lay on his bed, cooling down. The pillow was damp and the room dark when he finally sat up. Apparently Mom wasn't going to chase up here after him this time. Good. He was sick of, "Please, Mark, just cooperate with me," and "Things will settle down and get better, I promise." Things weren't getting better and they couldn't get a whole lot worse, he thought bitterly, trying to swallow the heavy lump in his throat. Everything in his life was wrong.

Mark paced the room, looking again at the old stickers his aunts had left marring the pine paneling of the walls. "Jellystone Park" and "Walt Disney World" and mini-maps of states like Arizona to California. The grandparents had taken their kids on plenty of vacations once; he'd never been anywhere.

Mark slammed his fist against a faded Jellystone Yogi sticker. It resounded with a hollow echo. The eaves were behind this wall, he realized, and looked for the entry. He'd gone into the narrow attic corridor once before, from his mother's room down the hall. The dusty space was filled with trunks and curling pictures and boxes of forgotten odds and ends that had stacked high in the century his ancestors had owned this house.

There, behind the bed. The paneling looked whole to the casual glance, but a close examination revealed the grooves of a long unused door.

Mark slid the bed away from the wall and found the tiny latch, heretofore hidden by the headboard. He pulled it, and the warm draft of stale air and dryrotted wood puffed into the room. He inhaled deeply, savoring the musty smell. The scent of treasure!

A half dozen open boxes of mouse poison were scattered inside the door, their contents slopped over onto the plywood. A sprung trap lay to the right. No still furry bodies, though. He stepped over the extermination devices, and felt along the wall for a light. A bulb hung near the door in his mother's room, so there should be one here as well. His hand grew sticky with spiderwebs, which he violently flung away. Then he found and pulled the string for the light. The bare bulb flicked to life, casting a sallow yellow glow across a burial ground of memories. Closing the door behind him, Mark sat in the middle of the narrow open space and looked around.

One side of the attic ceiling slanted sharply to the floor just a couple feet away on one side, while boxes and lamps and other odd items were stacked against the bedroom wall.

Eager to explore, he began pulling down boxes, and digging through their contents. Here was one with old dishes, chipped and covered with fine yellow fractures, but packed away nonetheless. Not like the grandparents would actually throw anything away, he thought with a shake of his head. Here was a box of newspapers, cracking with age. They were important headlines, he realized, finding a banner "One Small Step..." across the top of one from 1969, which lay atop another paper with a picture of a black car and headline screaming "Nation Mourns the Death of a President." Other, older papers showed veterans returning after wars, and one proclaimed a world series victory for the Chicago Cubs. Mark read the whole story in that paper, disregarding the flakes of yellow paper that fell like rust in his lap as he turned the pages.

In another box he found a strange collection of artifacts — ancient pictures of grim looking people, staring out of the thick paper-backed photos almost in challenge. *So you think your life is so bad? Try living in 1910*, he could almost hear them saying. Here was a more recent stack, with his grandparents before their hair had thinned and grayed. In the foreground lounged a girl of sixteen or seventeen, with long black hair and a twisted smirk on her face. His mother, he realized with a start. And she'd been pretty! A pang of unease tweaked his insides and he dropped the picture. But not before he wondered how that mischievous looking girl had changed from vibrant black and white to dreary color now?

He rifled through the box some more, finding radio tubes, a pink quartz rock, a pipe, and a cigar box. He pulled from the larger box and fingered the ornate lettering across the lid. "Dunham's Finest," it read. Would it still have cigars inside? He could take them down to the pond and try them out.

The lid opened with a paper squeal to reveal another assortment of valueless odds and ends. Hairbrush, fountain pen, belt buckle, more pictures, shaving razor, a silver Jesus medallion, a flute… A flute? Now that was cool…

It was gray wood, rough hewn and heavily veined in white and black lines. Hand-carved, Mark thought, fingering its short length. There were seven holes in its topside, each smudged dark with the wear of many fingers. The wood at the blowhole, on the other hand, was worn almost white from the saliva of past players.

He'd always wanted a harmonica, but a flute might be okay. His fingers sought the grooves of each hole, and lifting the wood to his mouth, Mark blew.

The flute gave a harsh honk. He blew softer and its tone mellowed to a plaintive, sweet whistle. He lifted his pinky finger, and then his fourth and third and index, running a stumbling scale on the tiny instrument. It was heavenly! Almost like the capering tunes he'd once heard at the Renaissance Fair.

The shadows of the attic seemed to lighten, and Mark closed his eyes, listening only to the music he was coaxing from the wood.

As his fingers grew more sure, lightly lifting and returning to their holes, he began to pick up first two at a time and then three, creating an almost classical melody. He squinted his eyes closed; the music seemed to dictate its own movement to him, through him. His fingers moved faster than he could think, trilling and fluttering, scaling and slapping the wood. The sweet tone vibrated through the eaves, through his arms and lips, into his head. He could almost see colors in its notes, smoky blue tones and feisty orange ones. Electric slides of violet and grassy tones of life and love.

He vaguely felt the clenched muscles of his belly and back loosen, and his heart seemed to pound surer. He thought, for the first time in weeks, not of anger, and why can'ts and sadness, but of sunlight and warmth and… girls. He held onto a girl's fleeting smile and concentrated on seeing the rest of her, on seeing her kissing him, on seeing her lead him to…

The flute's dance grew wilder as he concentrated on the dream and his hands grew hot. She was touching his shoulders, running her hands through his hair, drawing out aches and desires he only barely understood. And she was…

Real!

Mark opened his eyes and dropped the flute as the realization hit him. There were hands on his neck and lips on his head.

She was slim, fair-skinned, nude. He drew in a breath of surprise and embarrassment. She was the girl he'd dreamed, and yet not.

This girl fairly shimmered, the glow almost masking her nakedness, yet amplifying it. Her eyes were violet blue and seemed brighter than the dim light of the attic.

She knelt like a hazy dream in front of him, and before he could say a word she leaned in, took him by the shoulders, and pressed her pale lips to his own. His mouth tingled, like he'd tongued a nine-volt battery, but without the unpleasantness. He swam in the electricity of her kiss.

When she drew back, he allowed her to pull him towards her, and down so his head rested on her lap. She was cool, but solid beneath him. Touching a finger to his lips, she began running her hands up and down his temples. The ache in his heart drained with each stroke, and when at last he felt a glimmer of happiness, Mark slipped, unknowing, into sleep.

In his dreams, the glowing girl led him through forest trails, skipping and running, stopping to hug him, then dashing away. He followed, sometimes holding her hand, other times struggling to catch up as she tried to hide behind trunks and in brush. They kissed and rolled in honey-sweet flowers. They swam in a lake and climbed high in an old oak, so high they could look out and see the red and brown roofs of houses miles away. His heart flew; his feet were untiring.

"Mark, wake up and get out of there. It's time for dinner."

His eyes popped open from the lush green of the dream to the dusky glow of an old bulb and his mother's face peering in the doorway.

"What are you doing in here? You're liable to get bit by a rat or something. Come on."

He stifled a sharp retort as the peaceful cloud of his heart broke apart. There was no girl and no beautiful forest. There was only the steady patter of November rain and the dour expression of his mother.

His stomach filled with ice again. Dinner sounded like punishment. He picked up the flute from the floor and pulled the drawstring on the light as he followed his mother out of the eaves.

The table was ominously quiet as Mark picked at his roast pork and potatoes.

His grandmother could use a few lessons in seasoning, he thought, while the wet sounds of chewing and the harsh clinking of silverware around the table ate into his head.

He refused to meet their eyes, and they didn't try to

draw him out with conversation. For that he was glad. Usually, the grandparents would do their "smooth it over with small talk" routine, which generally ended up bringing on another fight. Maybe they'd learned their lesson.

In between bites, Mark glanced surreptitiously at the three adults, trying to imagine his grandparents without wrinkles, his mother with long hair. *How do people get like this?* he thought. He couldn't even grow a whisker, but his grandfather's face was pitted with dark and white stubble. *Do you just wake up one day old and cranky?*

He finished quickly, and excusing himself from the table, went upstairs to do his homework. Sometimes, even homework was better than hanging around his family.

Friday dragged on at school, and the storm of the day before left a chilly dampness behind. Mark avoided his mother Friday night and Saturday morning, but at last the ice broke during the afternoon. Once again he found himself screaming at her.

This time, she screamed back, "If you like your father so much, why don't you go live with him? Go on. There's the door. You're just like him, so you should have no trouble living with him. God knows nobody else could."

Mark stared at her, steel in his eyes. He hated her so much at this moment, he could reach out and…

"Fine, I will."

Pushing past her, he yanked open the door, grabbed his coat from the chair and stalked outside. It was another overcast day, and brown leaves puffed and skied along the ground at his feet in the breeze. Pulling on his coat, Mark walked down the wooded hill outside the house, heading for the pond. When he was younger, he'd caught frogs and tadpoles at the pond's edge while his parents had visited with the grandparents up at the house. These days, he moved along the pond's edge in distraction. There were no frog croaks to draw out his smile. He no longer practiced moving to the waters' edge in slow motion, so as not to alert his prey.

Mark sat down on the bank and leaned back against the rough bark of an old elm. All the mosquitoes and dragonflies were dead this time of year, and the cattails on the far side of the small pond were cracked and half-submerged from the wind. Mark reached inside his jacket to his shirt pocket and pulled out the flute. He fingered it gently, tracing the uneven whorls of vein in its grey surface. Turning it over, he saw it was detailed in filigree carvings. They appeared to be letters, but not of any alphabet he knew. Probably had belonged to one of his dead Irish great-greats, he thought.

Shrugging, he turned the flute over and held it to his lips. Would she come again? he wondered, and breathed a silent laugh at himself.

She hadn't "come" the first time, you idiot, he thought, shaking his head. Naked glowing girls didn't turn up because of old flutes. Unless you're dreaming, they didn't turn up, period.

Drawing a breath and placing his fingers, Mark began to play. Slowly at first, his fingers stiff with the cold. The wind seemed to pick up as the instrument's weak hisses turned to solid trills that leapt into the air, almost as if sound and breeze battled each other. Mark blew harder, and gradually, he felt a warmth spread through his hands and into his arms and head. The music grew more sure, his fingers more talented. Again he found himself closing his eyes, letting the flute guide him. Yes. The flute itself seemed to tell him what to play, what finger to pick up, what finger to flutter just so.

His heart screamed its anger into the flute, and into the air as the music danced, howling back at the howl of the wind, freezing out the cold of the day, reveling in the bitterness dredged from the pit of his heart.

He lost himself in the ascending, cascading, staccato melody. Again the insides of his eyelids began to dance with angry musical color.

Suddenly, something yanked him by the hair.

"Should be more careful with yer callin', boy," a black

voice growled in his ear. Mark opened his eyes wide and stopped playing. He lashed out with a fist at the monster that stood over him, but it only snatched his wrist in midair, crushing it in a painful grip.

The monster's thick, wrinkled trunk was black as dirt, with scabs of red and green mold trailing from it. Five stumpy arms twitched from its body, in addition to the two which held Mark by his hair and wrist. A single eye glared at him from a warted face. Its breath was worm dung, its touch, clammy mud.

"A toy such as that can get a tasty lad eaten by worse than the likes of me," the creature grinned, opening a maw as deep and black as a cellar door.

"I like games, boy. Do you?"

"Let me go," Mark gasped.

He was answered by a club to the head from one of the unused arms. "I said games. How about 'throw him in the river, see if he can swim, and if the Grogs don't eat him, throw him back again?'"

Mark's butt suddenly left the ground and the creature dangled him by his right foot over the still water.

"GRRROOOGGGGS" the creature shouted. The water beneath Mark's head erupted in a bubbling froth of leaves and mud.

Mark flung his body towards the bank. The creature pushed him away with another arm. Then, inch by inch, it began lowering him into the water. The icy cold of the water bit into the top of his skull and something started pulling handfuls of his hair in all different directions.

As his nose went under Mark screamed, "Noooo!"

And then he was ripped from the pond and tossed in a heap on the bank.

"Yer right," the troll mused. "Not a good game. Grogs are no fun anyway. Nothing left for me to eat when they're done. So tell me, boy, what eats your heart so black that you can speak to me? Not that I'm complaining, mind you, but it's always good to know where a meal's coming from."

Mark looked at the towering troll — or whatever it was — and grinned darkly. "You're not real. This is a dream, and I'm going to wake up with my bitch of a mother telling me it's time for dinner again, or it's time to go to that crappy school again, or it's time to do the dishes again. There are no fairy girls or trolls or grogs or magic flutes."

The creature showed a mouthful of stained and jagged teeth. "Foolish boy. Are you so blind? The world does not begin and end at your petty life. There are magics in the world you will never see, and creatures that could rip your mind to shreds with ecstasy, or pain. That flute you hold is a faery tool, and one hard to come by for a human.

It's more valuable than your life or mine, but you've used it to enter the hidden world and in yer entrance, broadcast yer pathetic bile to any in earshot. You're a mosquito, boy, and I'm gonna to slap you. But I always like my mosquitoes to know it before I suck their blood!"

The creature leaned forward and bit Mark's arm. Hard. Mark felt the skin break, felt the teeth sink into his bone. The pain was excruciating and he screamed once more, not realizing what he cried.

"Maaaaaa."

"Ha, ha, ha," the troll laughed, pulling back from his bite. "So you'll still call to the bitch if you git bit, eh? She can't hear you here, boy, but let's git a little more privacy, hmm?"

Yanking Mark by his bleeding arm, the troll strode up the bank, into the trees. Mark struggled, beating on the monster's arm, but the claws only tightened. It would break his arm in half!

At what Mark had always assumed was a beaver or muskrat hole, the troll stopped, and stepped a foot inside. When it disappeared up to the knee, Mark felt a sudden rush of nausea. The next thing he knew, the forest was gone.

* * * * *

They stood within a huge rocky cavern. Mark couldn't even see the ceiling, but the distant walls were lit with a greenish yellow moss. It glowed just enough to drape the air in a sickly twilight.

"Table's over there," the troll pointed. "If you'll just go lie down on top of it, I'll be right over to nibble. Need some seasonings, is what I've got to get. Don't bother trying to escape, you can't reach the surface without me."

The troll vanished into the murky shadow. Mark darted in the opposite direction. Reaching a wall, he realized the moss grew in patches. Splotches of cat's eye green grew irregularly here and there, thicker in some spots than others. He reached out to touch it, and drew back a finger cool and slimy wet. It looked like blood. Wiping it on his jeans, Mark followed the wall to a narrow unlit corridor. Checking behind him to make sure the troll was out of sight, he ducked inside.

The air here was colder, the chill running beneath his coat made him shiver. He was hungry too. And needed to use a bathroom. Mark suddenly realized he was more uncomfortable and scared than he'd ever been before.

His arm throbbed, and the sleeve, when he rubbed it, was wet with his own blood. That made his stomach queasy. Leaning against the cold rock wall, he slid to the floor.

The tears came easy, here in the dark, and he found himself thinking about the recent fight with his mother.

She was hurting just like him. But how could she just tell Dad to leave? Why couldn't they get along? *Stupid*, he chided himself. *You can't get along with either of them yourself, so who are you to talk?* He could do a better job at keeping his mouth shut, he supposed.

But she was so annoying. Fussing and fretting over him, telling him how to act and what to do. He was old enough to act how he wanted, and her smothering attentions only made him shove back harder. She was such a pill these days.

Where was that smirking girl on the black and white stoop now?

And where was the happy-go-lucky kid holding hands with both his parents and dragging them spastically from booth to performance to food stand at the Renaissance Fair just a couple years ago?

Thinking about that summer, he realized that his parents had been pushing each other away even then. Sure, he grabbed hands and held them together, but there were looks and words between the adults sharper than what seemed called for at the time. Maybe his hands had held theirs together longer than he'd ever realized. And now that they had split, he was pushing them both away from himself as well. Why did it have to be this way?

Pulling the flute from his pocket, he ran a finger across its surface. So cool, so small. And yet, magical. Had he been like this flute for his parents once? Small but magnetically magical? His music wasn't strong enough to hold them together anymore. Would the flute lose the power of its magic for him? Had he found a key to another world that would only grow useless and end up boxed in another attic someday, waiting for an unsuspecting child to uncover it? Would he even believe in its power tomorrow?

Putting the flute to his lips, Mark concentrated on imagining the girl he'd thought of in the eaves. He blew, softly, into the mouthpiece, and saw her violet eyes, her wan, knowing lips, her silken breasts. He pictured her running again with him through the fields, rolling in the fragrances of spring.

As he played, his mind strayed, the girl merged to the tender face of his mother, stroking his head as he lay feverish and sick in bed. She kissed his forehead and the ill feeling lifted slightly; the power of her love was great. And then she drifted away with a change in his music, and there was again the faery girl, stroking his head and kissing him with different ardor, and he tasted a different, equally-fulfilling love.

The bitterness washed from his heart at her touch…

Then he heard the bellow of the troll.

Mark opened his eyes to find the faery girl kneeling with him once more. Her wide eyes were sad and her hands gripped his wounded arm.

"He will kill you when he gets here," she whispered, her voice high and sweet. The troll's voice sounded near, bellowing, "Hide 'n' seek's yer game, eh? Boy, make me chase you and I'll eat you finger by finger, toe by toe. You'll be awake the whole time…"

"Can you take me back to the fields?" he begged her.

She shook her head. "You've brought yourself here, and you must take yourself out. Faerie is no place for humans — it magnifies your hates and loves so. You could lose your mind from each. I'm as dangerous to you as the troll."

"No, you're not," he said, bending slightly to kiss her. His lips tingled again at her touch, but she broke the contact quickly.

"Go home, Mark. Don't call for me or the troll again. Find a human girl, cherish your family. It all goes so fast for humans… Today you're young and spiteful, tomorrow you'll be old and bitter.

"Find another way; see the world as you saw it with me in the fields. Smell the life in the air. And go find it — in your world.

"Don't look for me. You'll play that flute someday and everything in your life now will be gone, you'll be old and dying, and I will still be as I am today. The troll will still be hungry. And other, more deadly creatures will be eager to heed the melancholy of your call. This is not a place for you. Use the flute now for the last time, Mark. Make it sing of the love of your family. Only you can create it. Go home to your life and live it."

The sparkling girl touched a kiss to his forehead and then, without pops or flashes of light to mark her passing, simply was no longer there.

Mark heard the troll's voice right outside his passage. Was he just supposed to wish his way out of this? If he blew the flute now, the monster would find him. Then again, if he didn't and the monster discovered his hiding place, he'd never get another chance.

Raising it to his lips once more, Mark pictured his grandparents' home. The photo of his dark-haired grandparents with a smirking daughter before them on the stoop of their house came to mind, and Mark found himself looking for those youthful smiling people in his dour guardians of today.

"So there you are, boy. Thought you could hide in the cracks did you?"

Mark blew.

The sound was harsh, rushed, fearful. He squinted his eyes shut and thought hard of his mother. Of her hugs, of her caring. It made him squirm to admit to himself that he did love her, that he missed her. He pictured the two of them walking, joking, kicking stones into the pond...

The flute trilled from flat, to sharp, to a major key. As Mark thought of the good times he'd had, and could still have with his mother, his fingers sped faster and faster. They burned with pent-up feeling, and just as he felt a gate open, in his heart and all around him, the troll grabbed him.

"Noooo you don't boy. Not escaping that way." A claw ripped his shirt.

Mark opened his eyes as he hit the top note of the flute's range. The troll slapped the instrument from his hand. The tip splintered in his mouth with a wayward whistle and flew up to strike against the ceiling. But with the sound of that last note, as the claws shredded his shirt, Mark also felt himself grow lighter, as if he were dissolving in the tune...

...and then he was standing, one foot in the muskrat hole.

He blinked, his eyes blinded by the greying dusk. After the green glow of the caverns, the edge of the night was as brilliant as noon. He pulled his foot from the hole, then looked for the flute. Had he lost it in the cavern?

There. A grey tube half hidden beneath a leaf. He grabbed for it, and came up with half the flute. Then he saw the other piece, a yard away. He pressed the two halves together and they fit without flaw. He hadn't lost any slivers. Crazy glue could join them, but could he ever play a magical song again?

Slipping both pieces in his pocket, he wasn't sure he ever wanted to. Life was tough enough without trolls trying to turn you into dinner. Though he'd like to see the girl again...

The warm, musty smell he'd always hated about the house seemed welcoming, not stale tonight as he pushed through the door and into the kitchen. Grandma was fixing dinner and her mouth dropped when she looked up from peeling potatoes at the sink.

"Mark, what happened to you? Are you alright?"

His mother's voice sounded from the front room. "What's wrong? Mark?"

She rushed into the kitchen, her face the mask of concern he recognized from so many nights when he'd been sick and she'd sat beside his bed. She came halfway across the room, then slowed, and stopped. She knew he hated her fussing, and she was trying to give him space.

"What did you do to your lip — and your arm?"

He touched his mouth and his fingers came away bloody. From when the troll had smashed the flute into his mouth as he played. It hadn't hurt until now, but it was swelling, he could tell. The pain suddenly hit him with a dull snap.

Kicking off his muddy shoes, he crossed the kitchen and threw his arms around his mother. Then he stepped back a pace.

"I'm fine, I just fell in a hole by the pond and got cut up a little."

He met her eyes then, and saw the love and pain mixed there. "I'm sorry about before, Ma. Really."

"So'm I, kiddo," she reached out and ruffled his hair. "Hey, your hair's wet, too!"

"I know, I know. The… um… hole had water in it. I'm gonna go up and shower and then I'll be down for dinner, okay?"

"Why don't you take off your shirt and let me look at that…"

"Ma…"

"Right. Wash up."

"There's alcohol and bandages in the linen closet," his grandma offered.

"I know. I'll be down in a bit."

He walked between the two women and down the hall to the stairs. And it didn't feel like he was escaping. For once, he thought as he climbed the stairs, he might enjoy Grandma's bland cooking. For once, this house seemed as wide as he wanted his world to be. Tonight, he might even be in the mood for some small talk.

Pulling the broken flute from his pocket, he stared at it for a moment. Then he walked to the bed, slid it away from the wall, and opened the door to the eaves. There was the box, barely visible on the floor a few feet away. He tossed the instrument, heard the pieces clatter to the bottom, then slammed the door shut.

He stripped off his clothes, wincing as his sleeve pulled at the already-scabbing arm. He hurried to the bathroom to clean up. He wanted to get back downstairs quickly.

For the first time in a long while, he was hungry.

Trick And Treat

The exit ramp for Willow Springs comes up fast, hidden as it is behind a copse of dense trees and brush, but I didn't miss it. Not with my eyes straining to see it for miles before I was even close. This was a rendezvous I desperately wanted.

Needed.

I hate to be alone on a holiday. Even a little holiday like Halloween. To sit in the dim yellow light of a living room leafing through the latest People magazine or watching "Talk Soup" on cable while in every house around you people are gathered together: lovers, families, friends... It's just too dismal to deal with. Thanksgiving, Christmas, Easter, the Fourth of July, and yes, even Halloween, I try to fill with company; anyone besides myself. This particular occasion was going to cost me cash to indulge my desire, but hey, if I wasn't paying for affection in this way, I'd be paying for it in another, right? Engagement diamonds, matching towels, a sofa set that didn't have sagging springs... So maybe this way was cheaper.

I saw her as soon as I hit the exit: long black hair flowing over an army jacket that stretched baggily to her knees. Her legs were provocatively bare from knees to her ankles which were protected in dark miliary boots. Her face gleamed bone-white in the headlights, which I flipped to parking lights only as I pulled onto the shoulder.

"Alex?" I called out the window, still safely belted into my seat.

She nodded and immediately moved to the passenger door.

"What'll it be tonight?" she asked, as she slid into the

seat beside me. I could smell her as soon as she opened the door, a sweet mix of jasmine and soap.

Good. I always worried about hygiene in these situations.

"I thought we'd drive up 41 a couple miles and pull off the road for a couple hours, if that's okay with you. There's a mattress in back."

She glanced into the back of the van and shrugged, apparently unconcerned.

"Fine. Two hundred dollars up front. And a guaranteed ride back here." Her voice was light as a summer breeze, but its tone was no-nonsense. I didn't counter. "Deal." I held out my hand and she gave me a tired smile; her grip was strong.

I pulled out the cash, and slipped in an extra fifty for incentive. Her eyes lit when she counted the cash and came out ahead.

"Let's go!" she grinned.

There's a great little side road off 41 that leads down into the woods and ends just a couple blocks short of the canal. The best part about the road is that the lone house that it leads to was abandoned when its owner died a few years back, and the "condemned" notice on the window, not to mention the rather predictable flooding it undergoes almost every spring, has kept any interested parties from snapping it up. The pavement is more like a gravel road these days than blacktop, as every year the ice and overflowing canal carry it away in chunks.

It was to this private drive that I took Alex for a Halloween date. It wasn't your standard holiday get-together filled with love and affection and Rockwellian warmth, but it was something. I wasn't sitting at home alone, answering the door to a bunch of barely-costumed teenagers looking for free candy every ten minutes.

As I turned off the engine at the end of the road, she made a show of unbuttoning her heavy khaki coat. I watched with growing excitement, catching glimpses of her pale skin through the opening of her coat. All at once she yanked it fully open, exposing firm white breasts and a beautiful dark pit of a belly button.

"Trick or treat!" she called out, and I must have blushed as her tits jiggled in the blue light of the dash.

She laughed and slipped the coat off. She was completely naked underneath, and I could feel my interest stirring. Or should I say rising?

"Actually, it should be 'and' not 'or,'" she announced, sliding closer, her flesh squeaking on my vinyl seats.

"Huh?"

"You're the trick and I'm the treat."

I had to laugh at that, but couldn't for too long. She thrust one soft, wide-rimmed nipple into my mouth almost immediately.

"What do you like, baby?" she purred.

I moaned a little, sucking harder on her nipple.

One cool hand scratched through my hair, coming to a stop at the back of my neck. She squeezed. "Tell me," she demanded, her grip uncomfortably tight. She had amazingly strong hands.

I broke away from the kiss, and looked up at her, embarrassment showing.

"I… I like to be told what to do," I admitted. "I like to feel nails and teeth all over my body. I like to feel… um, raped, kind of."

"Had a feeling," she nodded, looking not at all surprised. Maybe it was my extra cash or my red face. Whatever gave me away, my dark kink didn't phase her for a second.

"Take off your clothes," she said. Her lips were pouty and red — an incredibly sensual combination — but I could see in her eyes that she was bored by this routine. How many guys wanted her to slap them around then fuck them, like they were little boys being Mrs. Robinson-ed, to climax? I didn't want to know.

I did as she commanded, my heart skipping a beat as I

slid out of my jeans. My cock bobbed out of my underwear like a lazy dog's tail, and she grabbed me by its head. Not the most comfortable leash I've ever been on.

"Let's go back here." She pulled me, hard, to the bed in the back of the van, and pushed me down on the thin mattress.

"So you like it rough, huh? We can do that. Get on your hands and knees."

I rolled over, presenting my ass to her. She promptly met it with the palm of her hand. "I think you need to warm up a bit before we start anything."

I cried out at the next slap of her hand, reveling at the heat building in my ass and groin and spreading through my chest. My arms began to tremble.

"Roll over," she commanded, and I did. My view of the world darkened as she straddled my face and bent to lick my belly.

"Eat," she said, her voice growing throaty now. Maybe I was turning her on a little, even if it was only business. That made me glad — I liked to actually be friends with the company I kept on holidays. I could jack myself off anytime I wanted. Without human connection, that's all this would be — glorified masturbation. I wanted something a little *deeper* than that.

I felt teeth suddenly gripping my cock, and I cried out, the sound smothered in the musky, slick muzzle she held me in.

I bit back, and a tremor ran down her thighs. Her teeth moved up and down, scraping me painfully, and my desire grew.

Her nails began raking my ribs, and I twisted in that weird mix of masochistic pleasure and pain beneath her. I slapped at her ass, and she bit me back, harder. I must have screamed.

I was worried she'd broken the tender skin of my cock, but worry quickly slipped away. Fear was taking its place. I suddenly felt trapped, helpless. And her actions grew more violent. Her nails felt like tiny razors, slicing hard at my skin. I could picture tissue-thin strips of skin rolling off my body. I tried to push her off of me. I was getting scared, even as my penis grew harder. Don't they say that a man's cock is often at its hardest right after death?

This was too much, I couldn't handle it.

But her legs locked around my face, her nether lips seemed to loosen and kiss me deeper. My cock was engorged and powerful, thrusting on its own into the toothy heaven of her mouth. And just as I was ready to throw her from me with all my might, she released me, and came up to stare into my eyes.

"Now I'm going to fuck you," she announced. "Don't try to get away."

She sat down on me, and I could feel the sore spots on my cock where she'd chewed me. If I survived this little adventure, I was going to be walking funny tomorrow. But right then, those raw spots only made the pressure she was exerting unbearably hot. She raked at my chest with her nails, and now I saw them as claws, digging into me. I cried out, and I saw in her eyes the cruel flames of power, of lust. She was totally turned on by my pain, and I could tell from the set of her jaw that she wasn't going to stop. She wanted my blood.

Her head came down, her mouth wide open, and I could see the points of her canines. What had I brought into my bed? She buried her teeth in my neck, and I came, buried inside her. With excitement and sadness I realized that we had passed the point of no return.

Suddenly, I flipped her so that I was atop her.

Her eyes widened in surprise as she saw the glitter in my own. I mashed my mouth to hers, and her hands began raking my back — not in her powerful sadism of moments before, but in terror.

I couldn't pull back now. The sore spot on my neck from

her teeth sung in my veins, of mating and feasting, and the two within me were entwined. I bit off the tongue that was struggling to push me from her mouth. She tasted so good!

The hot stream of blood triggered my transformation.

Teeth extended, hands turned to yellow-clawed knives, I ripped open her throat as she screamed one short burst of terror.

I hope, at least, that she came before she died. I was too swollen with bloodlust to ask her.

I suckled her bountiful breasts briefly before chewing them off. Then I followed that sweet white trail from sternum to belly to dark musky delta. I thrust my snout back in where I had been so recently lapping as a man, bit off the tender flaps of her vulva. Oh, they were succulent. And her scent — ripe with sex and blood — sent my head reeling.

With one claw I poked at her deep belly button, and then with a hooking motion, ripped the creamy skin away. Oh, the meaty smell! I dove in as if she were a deep blue pool, slobbering with hunger as I rolled my head through her kidneys, feasted on the steamy coils of her entrails.

At last, sated in both cock and belly, I sat back on my haunches, and with some return of intellect, looked at her once more.

Her body was as beautiful now, still and shattered, as it had been mounting my manhood in frothy lust. Her limbs lay akimbo; marble-white death framed against crimson. I leaned forward to lick a spot of blood from her still pouting lips.

I hadn't wanted to harm her, but she took me too far. At the high point of passion, a man can't control himself.

And I'm not, after all, wholly a man.

I felt the beginnings of regret, as my teeth receded a bit, and my hands thinned slowly back to the type of fingers meant to peck on computer keyboards from the hooked claws meant to filet live dinners.

I sighed, looking at the hard beauty of her face. She had

been too good for her own good. I really had only meant to have a little sex and company tonight.

I try to reserve my wild holiday slaughters for Thanksgiving. But sometimes I can't control my instincts.

I backed the van slowly onto an overgrown path and down a canal loading ramp so that its rear end bubbled up with water. I thought that perhaps it was best that I didn't have a family to spend time with on holidays.

The noise level at dinner would be unbearable. And the mess to deal with afterwards! I also doubted if they'd consider it polite to fuck your food before eating it. Families can be funny that way.

I pulled the parking brake up, sloshed my way into the back of the partly submerged van and began using the slow current of the canal to help me clean up after dinner. The equivalent of doing the dishes.

Having company on the holidays can be a messy business.

After The Fifth Step

A fter the fifth step, it was mundane.

Ahhh… but getting to the fifth step. That was the trick. That was what it was all about. The crowds below, they thought the tough part was in the center, once the safety net was removed. "Oh, such danger," the ringmaster would cry. "Such daring-do."

Such malarkey, Reind thought. Once you were moving, in the groove, you didn't *need* a net.

The difficult part was in placing one step in front of the other when leaving behind the wooden platform. The first step was like a switch between stepping on sandpaper and high-gloss ice — with a slight movement, his foot left behind the immobile, grainy plywood to slip down a quivering, thin decline of twined, worn fibers. It was stepping through the door from plane cargo bay to open air. That step was the first trick. And the second, bringing your anchor with you.

The hardest was the step after the first. That's where you gained or lost your balance. That's where it became a walk or a fall. After the second step, there was no going back. You didn't turn around on the high wire.

The third step was a beginning. The first complete motion forward on a new course. The fourth step was an affirmation.

After the fifth step, it was just walking.

Reind put his first foot down on the tightrope and felt the horsehair fibers catch on the Lyrca net of his tights. Comforting feeling, that. While an unpracticed person would simply feel his foot slip down on a waving thread of uncertainty, Reind could feel his sole wrap and grip on the tightly-wound fibers of the rope. It wasn't like stepping on air. It was solid to him. Different than earth, maybe, but solid. If you were in tune.

Maybe that was the best simile. Walking the tightrope was like performing a violin solo. Long, elegant strokes across thin strands of fiber.

Of course, if you flubbed a note on a fiddle, you didn't end up so much dog food in front of an audience of hundreds. Usually. He thought of a spider, stepping without thought across skeins and strands of web.

Tarantula, sang a dirge in his mind from a long-ago album by This Mortal Coil. That's what he tread across. This Mortal Coil. A skein of filigree and shadow. The web of a tarantula. He smiled and hummed.

The second step fell true. He sighed, a breath of success. The audience didn't know the peril of those first two steps. It was the job of the ringmaster to keep them from focusing on that while the tightrope walker gained his composure and rhythm.

Down there, past the round, red-and-yellow-painted elephant step in the second ring. That's where the megaphone man made his plays. That's where the man with the handlebar mustache barked his exaggerated cries of, *"Can you believe it, he's about to step out on the wire without a net beneath him… quiet, ladies and gentlemen, this is very dangerous…"*

That was exactly when Reind didn't care anymore. That's where the danger became safe. Sleight of hand and misdirection were the calling cards of the circus.

After the first few steps, he was home free. The adjustment zone at the intro; that's where the tough stuff was. It was the job of the ringmaster to keep the audience focused on the center and the false bravado, where it was easy.

The third step was good, and Reind's heart slowed.

Oh yes. Even after all these years of walking, his heart

still kicked with a mule's petulant anger when he put that first toe to the wire. His mind may have been stubborn, but his body wasn't stupid. He knew that every walk could be his last.

But with step four, he knew that this was just another day. His bearings found, Reind moved steadily across the rope, one foot in front of the other, each step bearing down lower on the ever-so-slightly sloping rope, until he reached the center, and the object of the ringmaster's over-exaggerated cries of excitement. Once he started that upward incline on the far side of center (over the spot where there was no net) it was like walking up a hill. From the ground, it actually looked fairly level. But it wasn't, not quite. The second half of the walk was work, but it was easy. He began to think of Melienda, the night before. The way her fringed, gold lamé top had slipped from his fingers to the floor, a bouquet of tinsel. The way she'd shown him how a girl could really appreciate the controlled reflexes of a tightrope walker. She didn't care if his mother was the Three-Breasted Woman of the Freak Show tent.

She loved his surety of self. She loved his lips for their deceiving softness.

He loved her eyes for their kaleidoscopic play of spark and dark and mystery. He loved her dimples for their expressive blushes.

God, he hoped she didn't tell. This was a dangerous game. All of their other meetings had been during the break between their acts. They'd seen each other on the sly for weeks, but never had a night date before. When he slipped back into his tent to face Erin after midnight, he'd had to make up an excuse about helping Raymond with a faulty rope pulley. She'd yawned and shrugged, and turned away back to sleep. Did she suspect?

It was one thing for a man of the circus to love a woman of the same. It was another for a man of the circus to cheat on a woman of the circus with a woman of the same. He knew it was only a matter of time before someone talked to the wrong someone else. No matter how careful he was, tongues would wag. A circus was a family, and like any family, nothing stayed secret for very long.

Erin, Reind's wife, was a ticket-taker at the front gate. She had no 'talents,' but she'd loved the smell of the damp bales of hay and the heat of popcorn in the air and the sticky promises that pink cotton candy gave and the front gate cries of, *"Step right up ladies and gentlemen! Welcome to Barnett & Staley's Amazing, Mysterious, Phantasmagorical, Traveling Circus. Hear the mighty trumpet of the elephants and the happy horns of the clowns. Taste the taffy of our apples and caramel of our corn. Twist your body in the House of Illusions. And for the truly terrifying, visit our Freak Show. Come and see the frightening Mr. Lee. Dare to meet the stare of Felina of the Five Eyes!"*

That greeted the guests a dozen times a day in every town. They stepped past the ticket-taker girls and oohed and ahhed at the brightly colored, massive tents, at the fire-engine-red signs in the shape of giant hands that pointed this way and that, noting in daisy-yellow script: *"This way to the Freak Show. See the Three- Breasted Woman! Hear the tiny voice of the Midget Man!"* And another: *"This way to the Center Ring, the site of the Show of Shows."*

The people streamed inside the tent to see what they could never see at home. Sometimes, to breathe sighs of relief that they did not have such freakishness at home. But mostly to lose themselves in the strangeness and warped talent of it all.

The circus was ultimately about the people who came to see it. It reflected them.

And the people wanted to taste the salt of the corn and the sugar of the cotton and live the vicarious danger of a man on a tightrope and a woman in a skimpy top sticking her head inside the Man-Eating Lion's mouth. They wouldn't do it themselves, mind you. But somehow, seeing another person tread the wire or brave the teeth gave them

satisfaction in their own lives. That was what Reind did...
he gave satisfaction. He made life worth living for hundreds
of folks every day.

Erin had been one of those people, once. She'd come
to see him walk, and hung around after the show to talk.
She'd ended up in his bed. She'd asked if he minded, the
next morning. How could he have minded? She stayed with
him through the next town, helping out as they struck the
tents and pulled up the pitons and rewound the ropes. She'd
shown up in a "God Left Me for Another Man" T-shirt on
the third day with a backpack on her shoulder blades and
said, "I hope you've got room in your bunk in Cincinnati,"
because that's where they were going. He'd said sure. Aside
from the occasional fleas he ended up sharing it with (thanks
to the lions), he'd always give up space for a girl like Erin.

Cincinnati, Dayton, Cleveland, Minneapolis, Detroit,
Chicago... she'd been in his bed at the end of every show,
challenging him to walk a different thin rope than the one
he slid across in the air. This tightrope was wrapped in a
scrim of emotion and she was weaving it as they went. He
was trapped before they left Ohio.

She began to earn her keep at the ticket-takers' booths.

"I'll not have you carry me," she said, on the day that she
applied for the job. It's not like she had a lot of competition.
Most of the people who traveled with the circus had talents
and skills to show off. Or oddities. All Erin had were her
looks and a lover. And free time on her hands.

So she worked the booth.

Reind worked a tent.

They made the circus money, and moved from town to
town.

Until, in Peotone, Illinois, Reind met a girl with dark,
curly locks that stretched down to tease at the creamy cleft
between her purple crop top and the low-slung faded denim
of her jeans. And he slept with her in the tall grass just beyond the recently-mowed parking lot. And he found that

there was more than a wire, and a ticket-taker, and a suitcase to life. At least, that's what he thought, as her heavy, forceful tongue invaded his lips.

Reind thought he could quit the circus for Melienda, if that's what she wanted. He'd never thought that way when he met Erin. But for now, at least, he wouldn't have to consider it. Melienda had joined Barnett & Staley's Circus a few months before. She was the newest member of the family and was working in the Big Tent, ushering the animals and clowns and kids on and off the floor. Her name proved she didn't know how to spell, but she knew a whole lot else. In particular, she knew what made him feel real good. He'd found that out in between shows while Erin was still out at the front gate selling $3.75 tickets.

"Will you see me again?" she asked after, zipping up her jeans across bare pale flesh, flesh that was at eye level with him as he lounged on her wide cot.

"Yes," he smiled. "I'll do more than see you!"

Reind reached the middle of the rope walk and smiled, both at his memories of Melienda and his hearing the barker was bragging of how this was "the most dangerous fifteen feet ever attempted by man… a twenty-five-foot-high walk with no net across the deadly center floor of the Big Top." He could hear the audience take in a collective breath. Oooh. Ahhhhh.

His mind was far from the plodding step of toes to rope. His mind was on the deep, brown eyes and wide, pink lips of Melienda. And on what they might do for him tomorrow.

He almost didn't even hear the ear-crushing applause when he stepped up on the board on the other side and turned to bow to his audience, perfunctorily, before climbing down the ladder as a lion tamer came running across the dusty dirt floor to take his place in the public's eye. His private eye had other concerns.

Reind feigned sleep when Erin came in. He couldn't face her tonight. He was a terrible liar. And, truth be told, despite his feats on the tightrope, a coward. He lay in bed with his eyes locked shut, wondering if he could convince Melienda to stay in Springfield with him. The circus could pack itself up and hit the road, and when it arrived in St. Louis, it would just be short one tightrope walker and one glitter girl. They could hitch onto another circus easily enough. He didn't really believe the last part, and he doubted Melienda would either; she'd just finally ended a job search. How many traveling bands of multitalented gypsies were there in middle America? And how many needed performers?

He rolled on his side as Erin kicked her shoes into her trunk with two muted thuds, and slipped off her heavy, gold-lined, red jacket, draping it over a folding chair with a hollow clang of metal beads meeting metal back. As she did every night. He heard her jewelry hit the pressboard of her thin shelving unit. She insisted on keeping one light piece of furniture in their portable 'home.'

She slipped beside him under the covers, cool silk brushing his thigh. Reind could feel her eyes burrowing into his neck.

"You wanna talk about it?" she said finally. He didn't stir.

"Yeah, didn't think so," she whispered.

They both lay there, faces to the canvas ceiling, each knowing the other was awake, as somewhere a clock ticked through the hour, *click-stop, click-stop, click-stop, click-stop, click…*

When Reind woke up, Erin was already gone. Part of him was relieved, but another was frightened. What did she know? What would she say, when he finally came clean? He shook away the visions of her screaming and beating at his chest with clenched fists. He dressed quickly, and went out to meet the crowds. He had a show to do.

He passed his mother, Yvette, The Three-Breasted Woman outside of the Freak Show tent. Her arms were crossed over the objects of her attraction, and she shook her head at him and tsked.

"Behave," was all she said — though that was a volume for her — and vanished behind the flap of canvas.

Great, Reind thought. *Did everyone already know?*

The first step was harder than usual.

The second, almost impossible.

He couldn't focus. He kept hearing Erin ask in the darkness, "You wanna talk about it?"

She knew.

She *knew,* damnit. Maybe his mother did too! Shit, maybe the whole goddamned circus knew. But how? It hadn't been that long. And they'd been careful... Or was he just being paranoid?

He could feel a change in texture to the rope beneath his foot at step three, but didn't look down.

When you were on the wire, you didn't turn back and you didn't look down. But then he felt it again. His foot seemed to slide, just a bit.

Reind didn't move his head, but his eyes slid down, staring at the event horizon of the long rope below him. He saw the cause of the disturbance. If he hadn't been so preoccupied with his infidelity when climbing the ladder and starting out across the rope by rote, he couldn't have missed it.

Someone had wound strands of golden tinsel every few inches, all down the length of rope.

Cute, he thought, and refocused his gaze. Irritating, but not dangerous. He was already past step five and the rest of the way was just a walk in the park, really. He and Rafe, the tentmaster, would be having a long talk when he got down, for this little stunt. You don't mess with a guy's tightrope to 'pretty it up' without telling him!

Down on the main floor, the ringmaster was just winding up, getting into his act.

"Shh, ladies and gentlemen, be very quiet now," the man in the red-and-white-striped suit intoned, holding a finger to his lips. "He is coming up to the most dangerous part. A walk of intense peril. The most dangerous fifteen feet ever attempted by man... Look as he steps out over the ground fifty feet below... without a net!"

Reind hardly smiled at those familiar words. Old hat. He'd heard them too many times. He stepped, slipped a little again on tinsel, stepped again and stepped.

"Shit," he hissed. Something bit into his foot. He hurriedly stepped again and almost fell.

The rope felt as if it had disappeared and he was treading on a razor. The thin fabric covering the soles of his feet barely shielded them from the rope, allowing him to feel the texture of the strands beneath him. And right now, all he was feeling was pain and a growing heat down the center of his feet.

His arms struck out and waved for balance as his walk slowed, and the crowd took in its breath with a perceptible gasp. The whole world seemed to creak to a slow motion crawl.

He stepped again, and this time, cried out.

And again. The pain was growing, but Reind could not go back. He could not stop. On the wire, there was only going forward, or going down.

Reind looked down, afraid of losing his focus completely, but unable to stop himself from seeing what had been done to his rope.

His rope had been taken away.

Across the fifteen-foot gap above where the nets were withdrawn — the 'dangerous' part of his walk — a single, heavy steel wire extended. He had stepped, without seeing, from thick rope onto thin, slicing wire. Ahead, where the protective nets again began below, the wire rejoined the treadable thickness of rope.

He would not be safe until he'd truly walked the wire.

Tears were already slipping down his cheeks from the pain, but he would not, could not stop. To stop now would mean death. Or at the very least, a broken back.

Another step, and the skin of his feet was separating, slipping down in a wet, bloody kiss around the wire. He lifted his right foot, feeling the skin sucking at the steel as he pulled it up and away, only to place it down again.

He screamed.

And stepped.

Cried, "Oh my god, my god!"

And stepped.

The audience was aware that something wasn't right, and the background noise grew in volume as people pointed and chattered and a thousand voices whispered, "Oh dear, oh my."

He could feel the web between the second and third toes of his left foot give way with a painful tear and he nearly fell again, wobbling off balance, arms akimbo, waving from side to side but still his legs were not stopping, not slowing, no. He put his right foot down, bloody, shredded and fire-hot to the razoring foot garrote and swore every curse he knew in a foul blue stream, no longer caring if the audience heard or saw his moment of weakness. Now it was life or death for him.

This wasn't a performance.

This was a survival test.

This was a punishment.

At last the filleted remnant of his right foot came down on what seemed to be a foot-wide support of rope, and he pulled his left forward to match.

He'd made it. Whoever had done this, he'd beaten them. He'd survived.

He looked down at the familiar surface, checking to see if more foot irritants lurked in the last third of his journey across the sky of the Big Top.

The rope was free of exposed wire and golden tinsel. In their place, was a new decoration.

Every remaining foot of his walk was marked off with what looked like raven-smooth ribbons. Ribbons made of long, black twists of hair. The slippery, red blood of his foot was dripping down the satiny locks of one curl even now.

Reind knew whose hair had been shorn to decorate his rope.

Reind knew whose costume the golden tassels had been ripped and clipped from.

And when he finally reached the platform at the end of his faltering walk, when he slumped down on his knees to cry and shake with relief on the plywood surface, and saw the glass jar with a fist-sized, bloody organ floating inside, Reind knew whose heart had been cut out.

The doctor cleaned and stitched and dressed his feet, and assured him that he would be able to walk the ropes again. If he wanted to. Reind didn't ask about the new jar perched on the doctor's medicine shelf. The jar with something kidney-shaped floating inside.

Back at his trailer, Erin waited.

"They said you had some trouble with your walk today," she cooed, one eyebrow raised in an innocent question. "Oh my, what happened to your feet?"

He set the crutches aside and collapsed on the bed next to her, where she kissed his forehead and stroked his hair.

"My poor baby," she said. "Do you want to talk about it?"

Reind shivered and shook his head. "I don't think so. Some things just can't be said."

She stood up, shaking her head in agreement. "I'm glad you think so. I feel the same way."

She walked over to her shelves, and pulled a jar from the top. "Your mother gave me this today," she said, holding it out in front of her, as if to catch the light to see something hidden inside.

"She asked me what I thought about adding it to the display of two-headed calves and conjoined twins and all the rest of the twisted mutants they have jarred up over there in the Freak Show. I told her I thought so, but I said I'd ask you. What do you think?"

Reind took the proffered jar and stared deep within its yellow, formaldehyde waters. Inside, a tiny Tom Thumb floated, umbilical waving like a wrinkled, severed worm. Its eyes, barely the size of a pinhead, were black, and open. Despite its size, Reind could make out every finger and toe. It was perfect.

"Some things just can't be said," she murmured. "And some things just shouldn't be born."

Reind could see a tiny drop of blood hanging like smog near the tiny cord, drifting in the preservative. He choked, and nearly dropped the glass.

Erin rescued it from him, and flashed a sad, weary smile. "So what do you think?"

"I think it's going to be hard to walk for awhile," he said.

"Yeah," she answered. "Yeah, it looks that way. But you've got me to take care of you. We'll all take care of you."

She paused and met his gaze, her eyes hard. "We're all family, remember? The circus takes care of its own."

Then she took the tiny child and left the tent, leaving Reind to cry in dry, empty sobs over the loss of his son, and his lover, as he stared into the other jar left behind on Erin's traveling shelves. Reind stared for hours into the deep, brown, floating eyes of Melienda, who would never see again.

Seven Deadly Seeds

"You like to plant things, don't you?"

Bellinda looked up with a start from her digging. A moment before she'd been alone at the edge of the creekbed, plotting out her chrysanthemum garden in silence, with only the birds for company. Now an old woman stood nearby, her eyes cutting sharp as steel through the overcast of the chill spring day.

"Yes, ma'am," she answered, but offered no more. Mom had warned her not to talk to strangers. Mom didn't let her talk to *anyone*.

The woman stepped closer, then stooped to be at face level with Bellinda, dragging her thin black coat in the rich loam of the creek dirt.

"You know the creek overflows here 'most every year," the old woman warned, trailing a long red-painted fingernail through the dirt. "Your seeds may wash away."

"Dad said so, too," Bellinda retorted, "but my seeds are strong. They'll keep the creek away. And when they're big and have flowers, I'm gonna build a fort here and everything."

The woman smiled, her lips a thin pink scar across her weathered face.

"I could give you strong seeds to plant that would grow right in your house," she offered. "Then you could watch them every day, even when it was raining or the creek was high."

A light broke in the young girl's eye. "Really?" she asked in spite of herself.

"Sure," the old woman said. "What's your name, child?"

"Bellinda," the girl said. "I'm seven!"

"Well, Bellinda," the old woman said, reaching into a deep pocket of her coat. "My name is Penelope. And I have seven different kinds of seeds you can choose from."

She pulled her hand from the coat and opened it. The hand was wrinkled as a raisin, but in its palm were purple seeds pointy as a porcupine, grape-sized seeds red as hearts, sunny yellow seeds with pits like pecans and grass-green seeds that looked withered and sickly. But Bellinda's eyes lit when she saw the blue seeds. They were shaped like teardrops and glinted with the hue of a summer sky. She knew she shouldn't take candy from strangers… but seeds would be okay, wouldn't they?

"Those," she pointed. "I like those!"

Penelope nodded, and carefully extracted two blue teardrops from her hand. The rest of the seeds went back into her pocket.

"All right," she said. "You can have these. You have a root cellar in your house, don't you?"

Bellinda nodded.

"Plant them in the dark dirt in the cellar, then. But you must promise me two things. You mustn't tell your mom or dad that you've planted them, because they wouldn't like you digging down there. And when they've grown up and bloomed, you must bring me their seeds."

Bellinda nodded seriously. "Okay," she said. "How will I know when the seeds are ready?"

"They'll be ready when they look just like this," Penelope said, and dropped the two sky seeds into the girl's eager hand.

"Should I water them?" Bellinda asked.

"Only if you want. They grow on other nourishment. And they grow quickly, so watch them every day. You must bring the seeds back here to me before the plants die."

The old woman stood up then, her bones creaking with the effort. "Goodbye, Bellinda. We'll talk again soon."

"Bye," the girl said. Picking up her shovel, she abandoned the bag of chrysanthemum seeds and hurried through the long valley of shorn cornstalks that marched across her endless backyard.

Her mom, a thin, sharp woman in a faded pair of jeans and an orange and blue Chicago Bears jacket, waved from the sideyard where she was pulling laundry off the line. Bellinda cowered at the lifted hand, but then raised a small hand in reply. Mom was always slapping her for something, and since they moved out here to the country, she couldn't go anywhere to escape. She wished her parents could have moved away and left her to live by herself in their old apartment in the city. At least she had had friends there.

Bellinda didn't risk stopping — Mom would have found some reason to slap her if she got too close. Instead, she hurried up the wooden steps to the back door. Rather than going up the stairs inside, she ran downstairs to the root cellar. She wanted to plant her seeds before Mom came inside to see what she was up to.

She'd get a thrashing for digging in the cellar, she just knew it. So Bellinda quickly chose a spot in the far corner, where the boxes from their recent move were still stacked high. With her peach plastic beach shovel, she scooped away handfuls of sandy earth until she'd excavated a six-inch pit. Any deeper and the seeds would rot, Dad had said that when he'd shown her how to plant flower seeds. She didn't know if these seeds would make flowers, but she guessed that seeds were seeds and this would do.

The door upstairs slammed shut and steps clunked up the stairs into the kitchen.

Bellinda dropped the seeds into the hole and patted the earth back on top.

"Grow now," she whispered, and leapt up just as her mother called.

"Bellinda, where are you?"

She ran to her dad's workbench on the other side of the cellar and dropped her shovel on top. First grade had taught her a thing or two about setting up a lie.

"Down here," she answered, and then started back up the stairs.

"I was just putting my shovel away," she explained, when her mother met her at the door.

"Hurry up, then," her mom said, brushing a wisp of kinked brown hair out of her eye. "Go on and wash up. Daddy will be down for dinner soon."

Bellinda hurried up the stairs, turning over and over the sky-blue seeds in her mind. What would the plants look like? How long would it take them to grow?

Bellinda's parents were named Brian and Brenda, and like so many of the new residents of Faytown, Illinois, they were young Chicagoans who had moved to farm country to escape the crime of the big city. They wanted a quieter, slower life. And since Brian, an Internet web designer, could telecommute anywhere, they'd opted for this sleepy little corn-belt town. The ramshackle 1920's farmhouse — three stories tall and seemingly three blocks wide — had been a steal, and its upper attic had made a perfect office citadel for Brian.

The previous owner had disappeared a couple years before and the couple had bought the house from the town for back taxes. That meant that its old furnishings were all still in place, and Brian had just swept the loaded, dusty bookshelves upstairs clean and started piling his own books in place.

But the original occupants' tomes remained piled high in the corner, along with an assortment of vials, bowls, and small locked boxes. He intended to go through all of it before he tossed it, but their first month in the house hadn't given him much time for that sort of thing. The antique couches and chairs remained in place in the living room, as the couple hadn't had much furniture in their small city apartment. But the kitchen table was new, a white-tiled, blond wood-rimmed country table to match the house's decor. The family gathered around the table at 6 p.m. every night for dinner. If Bellinda wasn't in her place on time, she got sent to bed without any dinner at all. When that did happen, she thought her mom looked glad to be rid of her.

"You're always underfoot except when you need to be," Mom said.

On the night that Bellinda planted her seeds, Brenda served pot roast and mashed potatoes. She glowed with unusual cheeriness as she served it on the cornflower china.

"Now tell me if this isn't the best pot roast you've ever eaten!" she said as Brian cut into his meat and Bellinda forked up a thick creamy splat of potatoes. Mom didn't ask about Bellinda's pot roast. Mom said children should be seen and not heard. Bellinda thought she really meant that children shouldn't be heard or seen.

"I've got that Ryan Matthews over a barrel," Brian said, ignoring her boast. "He knows that he can't get a site put together without me. Not for the kind of money he wants to pay, anyway. Moving out here was the best thing I ever did. I don't have to charge Michigan Avenue prices now and they all know I'm the best. So if they want it done right, they can just sign on *my* dotted line." His chest seemed to expand six inches as he spoke.

"How's the roast?" Brenda prodded again. "I am just the *best* cook, aren't I?"

"Best one I married," he answered, dodging the question.

Brenda threw the fork down on the table. "What kind of an answer is that?"

Bellinda shrunk down in her seat. Mom was angry. It was best to be small when Mom got that way.

"You know the I-Food.Com site I did a couple months ago?" he said, ignoring her still. "It got an American Food Association award yesterday for best consumer design."

Brenda stood up. "How is your *roast*, Brian?" she said. It sounded like she was gritting her teeth.

He seemed oblivious to his danger, and started talking about a new javascript he was working on. When Brenda lifted his plate of food to slam it into his still-moving mouth, Bellinda chose that moment to duck behind her mother and tiptoe down the stairs to the cellar. Dinner didn't seem to be going well.

The cellar was dark and dank, as a root cellar should be. Its only light came from a single dim yellow bulb on a chain at the bottom of the stairs, and it smelled faintly of old apples and vinegar. The floor was hard-packed earth. There were shelves for canned foods all around the room, and they still held some spider-webbed bottles from the previous owners. Her dad's handful of shiny new metal tools stood out in easy contrast to the old rusted pliers and screwdrivers that littered the battered wooden workbench. Bellinda avoided the bench and shelves and hurried to the far corner of the room where she'd planted her seeds. She knew it was too early for them to sprout, but she wanted to see the spot anyway.

She was in such a hurry that she almost stepped on them.

Bellinda's mouth opened in a wide O when she saw the sprouts. Two pale blue tendrils reached up through the earth and yearned towards the plank ceiling above. They were already six inches tall. As she stared, they seemed to grow broader, their stems thickening and stretching taller. There was no breeze, but they shivered slightly. From the kitchen upstairs, Bellinda heard something crash.

"Wow," she whispered, ignoring the noise from above. "You're really growing! Do you want some water?"

Bellinda found an old mason jar on her dad's work bench and went quietly up the stairs and outside, careful not to let her arguing parents hear her. Then she filled it with water from the hose and returned to the basement. As she poured the water slowly over the plants, she could almost hear them sigh with relief. One of them seemed to twitch, and she saw that a palm-like leaf was separating from the stem. Her mother called. "Bellinda!"

She ran up to the kitchen, which was a disaster. The supper dishes lay shattered on the floor. Her dad was nowhere to be seen and Mom was crying.

"You liked your pot roast, didn't you hon?"

"Yes," Bellinda lied. "It was the best."

Her mom smiled at the compliment, sniffing and wiping her eyes quickly. "Go get ready for bed now. School's in the morning."

The next morning Bellinda tried to find a way to sneak into the cellar after breakfast to check on her seeds, but there was just no getting past her mom. "You're gonna be late, now hurry up there," her mom insisted, forcing a jacket over her sweater before sending her out the door to wait at the gravel road for the bus.

The school day seemed to drag on forever. Bellinda could hardly concentrate; it seemed the 3 o'clock bell would never ring. She wanted so badly to see how her plants had grown over night. Finally, the day was over and she ran to her house from the bus stop. Her mom was staring at herself in a mirror and combing her hair ever so slowly in the living room and never even looked up as Bellinda rushed by her and took the cellar steps two at a time.

"Wow," she said.

What else was there to say? The plants nearly touched the ceiling, and their skyblue fronds waved like alien palms across the back quarter of the cellar. Bellinda smiled as she stroked one of the leaves and saw that rows of teardrop-shaped kernels were forming at the edges of each long leaf. She stayed in the cellar until late watching the plants shake and grow, dancing slowly to an internal music.

When her stomach growled, Bellinda went upstairs to see about dinner and found the house was dark. The clock on the stove said 8:34. In the frontroom, lit only by the glow of a rising moon, her mom was still combing her hair in the mirror. But now she was wearing her New Year's Eve gown — a black dress lined with gold sequins. It was cut into a deep V in the back and a not much smaller V in front. She kept putting one hand on her hip and pushing her waist from side to side.

Bellinda opened a cabinet and found some Pop-Tarts and went unseen to her room. Mom didn't look like she was going to make any dinner tonight.

The next day when Bellinda got home from school, Mom was asleep on the couch and Dad, face black with stubble, cuffed her head absently as he grabbed a beer from the fridge and returned to his work upstairs. It seemed like he always had a beer in hand since they'd moved to the old farmhouse. At least he didn't yell and spank her much since they'd come here. She almost never saw him; he was always holed up in his office. Bellinda dropped her books on the kitchen table and ran downstairs.

The seeds were ready!

Bellinda knew they were done because they were so blue it almost hurt to look at them, and the pale blue of a couple of the palm fronds were already streaked with an unhealthy yellow. One by one, leaf by leaf, she plucked the blue teardrops from the two plants and stuffed her pockets with them. When the leaves were stripped bare, Bellinda had counted 27 seeds. She stepped back and looked at the monstrous plants and nodded. There were no seeds left to take.

The bottom leaf on one of the trees was now completely yellow, and as she turned to go upstairs, it fell to the ground. When it touched the earth, it evaporated, like a morning mist caught by sunlight.

As Bellinda watched, the center stems of both plants began to yellow and another leaf disappeared into the ground.

Her heart was full of wonder, and she ran out the back door and down to the creek, hoping that the old woman would be there to talk to. She had seeds for her!

When she got to the creekbed, she looked around at the silent cornfields and called Penelope's name. She barely had time to close her lips when the old woman stepped out from behind an old elm.

"You've done very well, Bellinda," the old woman said, as the girl poured seeds into her hand. "Did you get them all?"

Bellinda nodded, and flushed with her own flash of pride. Penelope had been waiting for her, just as she'd hoped.

"They grew so fast," she said.

It was the old woman's turn to nod. "Can you keep a secret?" she asked.

Bellinda's face lit up. "Oh yes!" she said.

"They're magic plants," Penelope whispered. "That's why you must be very careful when you plant them. And you must gather all of the seeds they produce."

"Can I have more?" Bellinda asked. "I'll be careful."

"Of course, dear," Penelope said. Her eyes glinted with pleasure and she once again offered a handful of colorful seeds. Bellinda pointed to the pitted yellow seeds and the old woman dropped two of them into her hand.

"Watch these carefully," she warned. "They grow even faster."

Bellinda thanked her.

"I'll be waiting for you," Penelope called after the girl, her thin smile lending another deep wrinkle to her weathered face.

Bellinda ran up the hill and back to her house with her new prize and thought of the strange things that had happened over the past couple of days. First she met the neat seed woman and then her parents started acting even stranger than usual. She wondered if the seeds had had some kind of effect on her parents. After all, they were magic. Then she shrugged. At least they were leaving her alone for once. It seemed like she was always getting her butt spanked and being screamed at. She would run away, if there was anyplace to run to, but out here in the country, she was trapped. There was nothing around for miles. She wished she could hurt them back; if only she weren't so small.

But now, they seemed to be doing their own thing, and she was doing hers. With a smile, she redoubled her pace so that she could plant her new seeds.

When Bellinda got back to the basement, all traces of the blue plants were gone. She dug a hole in nearly the same place to drop the "sun" seeds in the earth. Then she washed up for dinner.

That night Mom made dinner, but something still wasn't right, Bellinda found. Now Dad was acting strange.

"I'll take the beans," he said. "And pass the porkchops please."

Mom handed the plates to Dad, but she glowered at him. There were deep circles under her eyes and her hair was askew.

"Can I have the salt, please," he said. "And the salad."

Soon all of the plates were in front of Dad. As he forked and spooned the food into his mouth, he gave a wide smile. "This is the life," he said, apparently unconcerned that Bellinda and her mom had nothing on their plates.

"You know," he announced, "I got the Matthews account this morning. I told you I would. But I think I'm going to double my quote. He gave in too easy. He's got the money and I know it."

"Could we possibly have some pork?" mom asked.

Dad looked at her blankly. "You know, I think I'm going to go adjust that quote right now, before I forget." With that, he pushed away from the table and disappeared back to his office.

Bellinda and her mom rescued the food from his side of the table and ate in silence.

The next day Bellinda came home from school filled with anxiety. Her plants had sprouted last night, but again she'd been unable to check their progress after breakfast. She dropped her bookbag just inside the back door and ran downstairs immediately.

These plants were cool! They had elephant ear leaves that were dark green with sharp yellow spikes sticking out of them at the edges. And they were already three feet high.

As Bellinda looked them over, she heard a screech from upstairs. The plants seemed to shake violently, as if there were a strong wind blowing through the cellar, or a bird flapping in their fledgling branches.

Bellinda ran up the stairs to see who had screamed and stopped when she got to the kitchen. Mrs. Gailthen from next door was wrestling with her mom in the frontroom! She stood rooted to the tile as she saw her mom knee the older woman in the crotch and then push her to the floor.

"I've got to have them," her mom said, straddling Mrs. Gailthen. Her hands pulled at the earrings on the neighbor's ears.

Mrs. Gailthen screamed. "Are you crazy? You ripped my ears. You *biiiittch*!"

Bellinda's mom stood up and walked away, holding up a string of pearls to the light, and comparing the creamy stones of the stolen earrings to them. She didn't seem to see Bellinda as she took her new jewelry upstairs, leaving Mrs. Gailthen shaking her head in amazement behind her.

The old woman took a hand from her ear and screamed again as she saw the blood. "I'm bleeding, damn you! I'm bleeding!"

And then, realizing that only a child was listening, she hurried from the house.

That night after Bellinda had tucked herself into bed, a shadow leaned across her bed. Peeking unobtrusively from the security of her blanket, she watched as the shadow moved across her room to her dresser. Something rattled and something else fell to the floor, but she didn't let out a sound. What if it was looking for her?

But the shadow didn't come for her, and soon it disappeared, closing the door behind it.

JOHN EVERSON

When Bellinda got up in the morning, her piggybank was missing.

She cried alone in her room, knowing that to complain about it to her mom would only end up with her getting spanked somehow. But she'd had five dollars and thirty-four cents in there! She'd been saving for weeks.

After school, Bellinda once again ran to the cellar and screamed with delight at the size of her new plants. Their leaves were as wide as her kitchen table and the plants' tops strained against the ceiling. Each of the leaves held dozens of spikes, and at the tip of each spike grew a thick lemon-drop of a seed.

"Bellinda?" Her dad called from the top of the stairs. She ran up and met him in the kitchen. "I'm glad you're home, baby," he said.

"Where's Mom?" Bellinda asked. Even though he worked at home, it was odd to see dad in the middle of the day.

"Well, that's why I'm glad you're home. You know how I always tell you not to take the candy at the store without paying for it?"

She nodded.

"Well… Mommy forgot about that rule and now she's in trouble with the police. So I'm gonna go down and help her out."

"Mommy took candy without paying?" Bellinda asked.

"No, honey. She took diamonds. Can you stay here and work on your homework while I'm gone?"

She nodded again and he patted her head.

"Good girl. Don't get into any trouble, now."

Bellinda was happy to have the house to herself. Lately, when her parents bothered to notice her, it was only to yell, so the quiet was refreshing.

After her dad left, she went back downstairs and saw that her new plants seemed to be wilting. She took the mason jar and went outside to get water for them, but when she

90

came back downstairs, she noticed that one of the two tree-like plants had a dark brown streak down its leaves. As she poured the contents of the mason jar on the ground at their bases, something plopped to the ground behind her.

Then again.

The seeds!

The floor was already littered with a handful of the sunseeds. Bellinda remembered how Penelope said it was important to get all of them. She picked up the fallen ones and dropped them in the jar. Then she began to pluck the remaining seeds from the leaves.

When the mason jar was full, she stuffed the rest in her pockets. As she plucked the last one, the entire plant seemed to shudder and fold in upon itself. She squeaked and jumped backwards as the elephant trees simply sunk into the ground, disappearing with a whisper of sunny dust fogging the air.

Bellinda ran all the way to the creekbed and called Penelope's name before she even neared the large elm where she'd last seen the old woman.

Sure enough, Penelope stepped out from behind the tree.

"Are they ready so soon?" Penelope asked.

"Yes," Bellinda said breathlessly. "And they made so many seeds."

"You've been a very good gardner." Penelope patted the girl's head. Bellinda felt warm all over at her touch.

She decided that Penelope was no stranger, and it was definitely okay to talk to her.

"You said the seeds are magic?"

Penelope nodded slowly. Her black cloak fluttered ominously in the slow wind.

"Is that why my parents have been acting so weird?"

Again, Penelope nodded. "The seeds grow on the sins and desires of your parents. And just as the dark souls of your parents feed the plants, so do the plants feed the dark in your parents' souls. And the result is that you and I get more seeds."

Bellinda grinned. "You're a witch, aren't you?"

Penelope said nothing, only arched an eyebrow.

"I want to be a witch like you," the girl ventured. "Then my parents could never hurt me."

She looked at the seeds remaining in Penelope's outstretched hand and said, "Which ones are the strongest ones?"

The corner of Penelope's mouth turned up and she pointed at the red seeds. Bellinda nodded once and said, "Then I want those."

"The old woman showed all of her teeth as she handed them over.

"These are very powerful," she said. "You come get me if you have any trouble."

The heart-shaped seeds grew fast, and Bellinda skipped dinner again to watch them. But this time it wasn't because she was more fascinated in the plants than dinner, it was because Mom and Dad were playing naked on the kitchen table. She'd made the mistake of coming upstairs when she heard the noise, but quickly slipped back downstairs when she saw what they were doing.

Her new plants were covered in small thick, crimson leaves. Each leaf was like a fat circle of deep green flesh covered with fuzzy red velvet. Bellinda enjoyed running her fingers across them. They tickled, but that felt good, too.

After things in the kitchen had quieted down, she carefully crept up the stairs to make sure Mom and Dad had left. They had, but when she went to her room, Bellinda could still hear them giggling and crying out in their room down the hall.

She closed her door and went to bed without supper, again.

The next day, when Bellinda came home, the seeds were ready. She ran downstairs without stopping to see them.

But her excitement about them was tainted when she walked into the front room and found her mom lying on the floor.

Mom wasn't wearing any clothes, and her arms and legs were twisted around the naked body of the mailman. He had dark black hair and a pimply butt. Bellinda knew it was the mailman because his U.S. Postal bag was lying on the floor near the door, along with his clothes.

Dad — who still had all his clothes on — lay next to them with a silver gun in his hand. All three of them had blood leaking from their heads. It bloomed in bright crimson petals on the pale carpet.

Part of her was relieved; they wouldn't hurt her anymore. But part of her was scared, too. Bellinda didn't know what to do; the only adult she knew in this town other than her teacher was Penelope. As soon as the thought of the older woman crept into her head, she smiled. Penelope would know what to do.

"Back so soon?" the old woman asked.

Bellinda nodded, tears streaking her freckled cheeks.

"Mommy and Daddy are dead," she declared. "And the mailman."

Penelope nodded. "The seeds of lust can work strange things on a couple," she said. "And with the aftereffects of the seeds of pride and greed still in the air... well, I must say I'm not surprised. Did you collect the seeds?"

Bellinda shook her head no, and Penelope patted her on the head.

"Well, then we'd best go do that, and while we're at it, we'll see if we can't clean up the mess they've made. They did stain the carpeting, I bet, didn't they?"

Bellinda thought of the pools of blood surrounding her parents heads and nodded, one tear trickling down her left cheek.

"I thought I'd heard gunshots earlier. Well, come on then."

Together the two descended the cellar stairs and plucked each fat red seed from the cone-shaped sprouts of the velvety plants. There were only a couple dozen of them, but they looked thick, bloodfilled and healthy.

Then they went upstairs.

"Stay back," Penelope cautioned, and ventured alone into the living room.

Bellinda sat at the kitchen table as Penelope reached into her black satchel for a vial of something dark. She opened the stopper, blew across its mouth and mumbled some guttural phrases that sounded like nonsense.

When she was done, Bellinda smiled at her and took her hand. It was cold but firm.

"They weren't very nice," she said and followed the witch upstairs. When she did, Bellinda noticed that the bodies were gone from the living room.

In the upstairs office, Penelope used one arm to brush the row of Dad's brightly colored books from the shelf onto the floor. Then, one by one, the old woman began to replace them with her herbal and occult books — some bound in crusty leather — from the dust pile in the corner of the room. Finally, they were back on the shelf where they had been before Brian's brief ownership of the room.

On the lower shelves, she set the dark old canisters.

She opened an empty one, and poured the blood red seeds and closed the lid tightly.

"Are those things all yours?" Bellinda asked.

"Yes," Penelope said. "I've been waiting to get them back. But first I had to leave this house so that a new family would move in and bring me an assistant."

Penelope held up a canister and Bellinda could see within it a handful of grey seeds that looked almost like garden slugs. They were different from the ones she'd planted in the cellar.

"I planted some of these, my own magic seeds, before you moved in," the older woman said. "Thanks to them, your family moved into the house. I think your parents brought me a good harvest."

"You used to live here?" Bellinda asked.

"Oh yes," Penelope smiled, cupping the girl's chin. "When I first came here, I was a little girl just like you. And I met an old woman who gave me seeds to plant in the cellar, too. After they grew, and my parents went away, the old woman moved in and took care of me. She taught me all about growing all sorts of special seeds, and other things."

"She was a witch, too?"

Penelope nodded. "Would you like to learn magic?"

"Will we plant the rest of the seeds?" Bellinda asked. "If I could plant them by the kids at school, I bet they'd grow really fast."

"Not here or now," Penelope said. "I think we've grown just about enough deadlies for this week."

The girl's mouth puckered slightly, but then she brightened.

"Are you gonna stay here with me? Will I get to become a witch like you?"

Penelope gave her a crooked smile. "If you like."

Bellinda nodded once and then disappeared from the room for a moment. When she returned, she was wearing a long black sweater of her mother's. It dragged on the ground like a dress and bunched in comical thick folds at her wrists. But when she stood next to Penelope, the light from the room seemed to fade into cold shadows.

"I'm ready," the girl said.

Preserve

I don't kill, I preserve."
He smiled reassuringly.
I knew I had come to the right man.

The man was Arthur. He put the art in Art's Taxidermy, a tiny little shop around the corner from Main Street. You'd miss it if you didn't know it was there. The shop squatted in one of those old white Victorians converted to businesses when people grew more inclined to shop, rather than live, downtown. Like most of the converted homes in the area, the only clue to there being a business, instead of a family, inside was the shingle hung near the sidewalk: Art's Taxidermy.

I'd heard the rumors that Arthur did more than stuff nine-pound bass and mount deer heads for the overly proud hunter's den. They said he'd embalm a man – if the price was right. The only problem was in getting the body. I intended to make that part easy.

"My life savings," I said, holding out a bank envelope containing a not inconsiderable sum. I had withdrawn it less than an hour before. "It's yours; I won't need it."

He shook his head slowly. A silver cowlick bobbed with the motion. For the second time he insisted, "I don't kill, I preserve."

He hesitated a moment. I could see worry lines wrinkle near his eyes. "Let me show you."

Arthur stepped out from behind the glass counter he'd been working at when I came in. He was slender, bi-focaled, sixty-ish, about my height – five-foot-nine. He locked the entrance door and turned around the sign in the window.

Now the *Open* sign faced us. I was hoping he'd be amenable to opening a vein. The menagerie of stiff squirrels, beavers – even a skunk in one corner – demonstrated his prowess with filling veins.

I expected the baby deer that stood poised to jump on the far side of the room to do so at any second. They all seemed so… alive. As if he and I existed outside of a second in time – while they were trapped inside.

It reminded me of Caitlin. *I really didn't mean it*, I said to myself for the millionth time.

"This way."

I broke my reverie and turned to follow Arthur, who was waiting in the hallway for me to follow.

He walked stiffly through a 1950s style black and white tiled kitchen, pausing to open a door next to an old refrigerator. A pile of fresh rabbits' feet were staining the white formica snack table a dark red. I must have frowned when I saw them.

"Disgusting, isn't it? To dismember an animal – for luck! But people bring them in and people come to buy them." He shook his head. "I would rather preserve the animal in its full form. As beautiful in death as in life."

He motioned for me to follow and disappeared through the door. Twelve creaky steps and I was standing in an old stone basement, murkily lit by one bare bulb. A cord ran from the light to the top of the handrail upstairs. The walls appeared to have been chipped out of solid bedrock. I shivered from the icy damp air. Arthur headed to a door in the south wall to what seemed to be a fruit cellar. My grandmother had had one like that in her basement. He slid back the oak door and we both stepped through.

It was a dollhouse.

A dollhouse on a real-life scale. The floor, ceiling and walls were rough hewn wood, elegantly decorated with persian rugs and ornate tapestries. A scarlet shaded hurricane lamp lit up part of the room, which extended much farther than any fruit cellar should have.

But fruit was not what Arthur was keeping. Arthur's dolls were people. Had been people. They were everywhere – on divans, leaning against the walls, lying seductively on the floor… It looked like a snapshot of a nudist convention in a 19th century sitting room.

"What do you think of my friends?" Arthur asked.

"How…"

"They came to me, as you have," he said softly. "They begged me for death. I promised to preserve them. I kept my promise."

His steps thudded on the planks as he crossed to a shiny mahogany victrola. Cranking the arm of the machine like he was winding up a Model A, he continued talking to me over his shoulder. "Jeanine loved the big bands."

He set the needle down on a thick black platter, and the scratchy clarinets of Benny Goodman's orchestra echoed through the room.

"This is Marshall," Arthur announced, patting the shoulder of a youngish man propped up at a small table on his elbows. His naked, fishbelly white and nearly hair-less legs were delicately crossed beneath the table. Arthur turned the page of a Bible resting between Marshall's arms.

"Marshall said he'd never been able to read the Bible cover to cover," Arthur said quietly. "Now perhaps, he can."

I didn't think Marshall was in much of a state to read anything. But his eyes seemed to glint as Arthur crossed behind him and bent over to adjust a knob on a machine beneath the hurricane lamp. It hummed a bit louder after his touch, and I noticed tiny tubes ran from it to each of Arthur's "friends."

"This is what keeps everyone looking so nice," Arthur explained. "If you could see the skins under the pelts of the animals upstairs, you'd see how it gets sunken, wrinkled, dis-colored. Everything settles in. So with humans, if we don't want them to look like mummies, we pump them up with this solution here."

He walked over to a blond woman arranged seductively on a purple velvet couch. If her skin hadn't had a disturbingly bone-white caste, she could have been a *Playboy* centerfold brought to life.

Her eyes were half open, her lips – painted with bright red lipstick – were parted. I felt like a necrophiliac looking at her. She excited me.

"Touch her breast," Arthur commanded.

Why not? I thought. *Pretty soon it won't matter anyway.* Still, my arm shook as I gingerly fingered a rouged nipple. It was cool, dry – and seemed to ripple as I took my hand away. Arthur reached between her legs for a moment and his face took on the relaxed aspect of a man stroking his pet cat.

"She could never get enough," he said. "That's why she came to me. There wasn't anything that could satisfy her."

He reached into his pocket and pulled out a silver vibrator.

"Still, I try for her," he whispered. A low hum filled the room and I turned away.

"Why do you want to die?" he asked.

"I just can't stand to live anymore," I answered. In my mind I was picturing Caitlin's frozen look of surprise as she fell backwards from the landing. I'd been violently angry, we'd been punching and screaming at each other, but I'd never meant to kill her.

"Certainly that will pass," Arthur murmured.

"No." I said, equally quiet. "It certainly will not."

"Why not take your own life, if you cannot stand it so much?"

My hands grew damp instantly at the suggestion. I thought of the thin blade jutting crookedly from Caitlin's side, and the amazing spray of blood. In the heat of the moment, after she'd kicked me in the thigh, I had grabbed the steak knife off the counter to force her to back off. But she was already in motion, and the knife slid into the new scabbard of her flesh with almost no resistance. She might have survived the wound if she hadn't jerked away and stumbled backwards over the low banister. I could still hear her neck snap when she hit the tile foyer below.

"I just… can't."

Benny Goodman had ended; the needle was rubbing against the record label in a comforting, rhythmic fuzz. The humming abruptly stopped, and Arthur turned off the Victrola.

"Come with me," he said, and we left the dollhouse behind.

He took me to a long steel table on the other side of the basement and switched on a fluorescent ceiling lamp.

"Take off your clothes and lie down."

My stomach twisted at the thought of getting naked in front of this man, but I chided myself once more. *It's like dropping your pants for the physical*, I thought. And it certainly didn't matter at this point.

"How will you do it?" I asked, stepping out of my jeans.

Arthur pulled a machine out from a cabinet. It resembled the one in the dollhouse.

"Well, we need to drain your blood, but we don't want anything to clot up and sink, do we? We also don't want any unsightly gashes to mar the body. So, I'll just pop this IV tube into your arm like so…"

I winced as the needle pricked into my skin.

He nodded. "It will be uncomfortable at first, but soon you'll just get sleepy. Don't fight it."

Holding the end of the tube shut with his thumb, he walked over to a sink behind me. I heard something flop inside, and felt a tugging sensation as my blood started to gush through the tube.

He's funneling away my life, I thought, somewhat incredulously, but with relief, not fear. Soon it would be over. The nightmare, ended. If they found Caitlin, they would certainly not find me. Who would think to look in a taxidermist's basement?

"Now after we get rid of most of this blood, I'll be flushing you with this solution," Arthur said, dragging the machine around to my unencumbered arm.

I was starting to feel uncomfortable and cold. I could hear my heart pumping. It seemed to be getting louder. Struggling maybe, to keep up the pressure. *Good luck*, I thought, and smiled.

"Will you miss anything?" He seemed to be talking from very far away.

"Rachmaninoff," I mumbled. "I'll miss playing Rachmaninoff."

"You are a pianist?" he asked, leaning over the table to stare into my eyes.

"Uh huh. Could've been... uh... concert class. But... Caitlin... Uh, needed money, not music."

I giggled.

Now she didn't need either. And neither would I in a few more seconds.

"We both... lose," I said.

Arthur's face looked pained. "She may come back, you know."

I had told him upstairs that my wife had simply disappeared one day. "No, she won't," I gasped.

The room was getting hard to see, and my legs started thrashing.

Arthur clipped a belt across my legs, and then cinched down both of my arms to the table. "I think it's time," he said.

I felt the needle enter my other arm. The pump kicked on and I was blinded with cold. It shot up my arm like a white hot icicle. My fists were clenching, pounding the table. My head rocked from side to side as the bitter stream raced through my body. I could feel it travel. Inch by inch, my body was tingling with its touch.

I closed my eyes and silently said goodbye. At last.

* * * * *

So you can imagine my surprise when it dawned on me that I could hear Rachmaninoff playing. It was scratchy, but without a doubt the glorious allegro to his Symphony #2 in C minor. Was there really life after death, I wondered?

But I still felt frozen. Could Dante have been correct? Did I really warrant the ninth circle?

"Good morning everyone."

It was the gentle voice of Arthur! Certainly Arthur was not the devil. Devil's advocate, maybe.

Somewhere a pump accelerated in pitch.

How. How could I be hearing this? *I'm dead!!!* I wanted to scream. I mean, I *really* wanted to scream.

Suddenly the haze in front of my eyes lifted. I was in the dollhouse, sitting on a bench. My hands were poised on the keys of a Steinway baby grand. Arthur was making his rounds.

"I'm so sorry about your lover," I heard him say. He was running his hands across the chest and pelvis of a skinny blonde kid who looked like a frat boy.

"Does this feel better?"

I wanted to look away, but I couldn't move. I couldn't turn my head, close my eyes, scream – nothing. Except see straight ahead. Arthur stepped towards me. I was like looking at someone through a photographer's fisheye lens. His face grew grotesquely large and distorted as his lips brushed my forehead. I realized with increasing horror that, while I couldn't move, I could feel. His kiss left a faint, but noticeable, tingle.

"I hope you like the piano, Richard. I know you can't play, but perhaps just sitting at it, and hearing Rachmaninoff..." his voice trailed off.

Behind me a low hum started up.

That's when she walked across my line of vision. A sad looking wisp of a girl, all in black.

"Touch her breast," I heard him say familiarly. "She likes that."

"But she's dead," the girl answered him. "You killed her." She sounded awed.

"I never kill," he replied firmly.

"I only preserve."

Hard Heart

Tricia tugged at the heart on her sleeve. Her face wrinkled in complaint, but after awhile, it came loose, ripping from her arm with a sound like Velcro separated under water. She held the heart with pincer fingers, avoiding its clumsy pulsing attempts to reattach itself.

"Would you take this?" she asked the boy sitting at the other end of the bench from her. "I don't want it anymore."

His name was Mark Fisher, and his sleeve was not marred by any such organic accoutrement.

Mark scratched the back of his head. "It's kind of gross," he said quietly. "But it's also kind of cool. Sure, I'll take it…"

Tricia surrendered the drippy organ to the soft-spoken boy.

She'd seen him sulking around school a lot, and earlier had decided he'd be just the kind of sucker who'd accept the harness of a heart.

Let him, she thought, watching him toy with the steadily throbbing muscle. It climbed up his arm, a centimeter at a time, coming to rest just above the elbow.

She felt a strange hollow pain her chest and throat when a smile crossed Mark's face. Determined to enjoy her new freedom however, Tricia skipped away, leaving her heart in the hands of the grinning boy.

Tricia thought she'd be ecstatic about getting free of the heart on her sleeve, but the farther she got from the bench where she'd left it, the slower her steps became. It had been a burden, she reminded herself – always announcing to people it was there, making it difficult to blend into a crowd, getting her into trouble in school and with her parents because of its compulsions — she was much better off without

105

it. But as she answered the bell to return to class, her face hung listless, her arms dangled limp as muslin drapes in a house with no windows.

"Hey Trish – you wanna come over today after school?" a voice called from down the hall. Sally Ketchal, the most annoying kid in class. Tricia had found excuses for not going home with Sally a hundred times this year, but now she found her mouth dry of words. She shrugged and nodded.

"You will?" Sally squeaked. Tricia winced inside, but said nothing. "Great! We can play Barbies and maybe my sister will make brownies and…" Sally chattered beside her all the way to class, but Tricia didn't hear a word.

In Tricia's head, over and over, she listened to the slurping, tearing, horrible sound of the heart leaving her sleeve – and wondered why it had taken her will with it.

Math class seemed to drag on forever. Until something strange happened: Mark Fisher actually *raised his hand and answered a question.* She couldn't remember ever hearing him speak in class before. But now, as he did, she saw her heart — now *his* heart — beat faster in satisfaction.

That night, Tricia tried to remember why she had wanted to give away her heart. From the moment it had left her arm, she'd felt empty — and bad things kept happening to her.

Mrs. Engelbright had called on her in class and she hadn't been able to spit out the answer. Everyone around her smirked and whispered. Then she'd had to endure the inane prattling of Sally all afternoon because she couldn't seem to open her mouth and change the subject, say shutup or anything. It was not a problem anyone would have ascribed to her before. And then, to top it off, she'd gotten grounded for being late to dinner. Instead of wheedling her way out of it as usual, she'd glumly accepted her punishment (as her parents passed each other sideways glances of shocked surprise).

Mom had lectured her over and over about not speaking her mind to any and everyone, but Tricia had now come to the conclusion that letting her heart rule her head was tons better than having no heart at all.

Lying in bed with tears dampening her pillow, Tricia decided she had to get back her heart, loud obnoxious ornament that it was. Without it, she felt as free as a lion in a cage.

* * * * *

"Hi Tom!"

Tom Harris looked up from the comics rack in surprise. It was that dweeby quiet kid – Mark. What could he want?

"Have you seen those Anne Rice comics they've got about that vampire? They're really cool."

"Yeah," Tom grunted. "I've got 'em all."

"No way!" Mark gushed, oblivious to Tom's leave-me-alone stare. But Mark's newfound enthusiasm was infectious, and the Anne Rice series was one of Tom's favorites. Soon they were interrupting each other in excitement. By the end of the day, they were fast friends.

* * * * *

The following day during lunch recess, it was Mark who found Tricia, sitting silent on the bench outside. Their positions weren't totally reversed – he was not there to trade away his newfound heart.

"How ya doing?" he asked, with a cheer Tricia remembered once being her own. "Okay," she replied, but her eyes seemed far away. Trapped inside her ribs a voice was yelling, *"I'm horrible, I want to scream, I want to cry and I can't open my mouth! Please, please help me!"*

But she only smiled sadly.

"Are you still glad you gave this to me?" he asked a little guiltily, pointing at the bright blob on his arm. He didn't want to give it back, but he knew it must be pretty valuable.

It was a very forward question for Mark, but he felt good asking it.

Tricia nodded, but Mark noticed the gleam in her eyes. She looked away, but not before he saw the tear tracing a slick path down her cheek.

He wanted to turn and run. His heart skipped a beat. She *did* want it back. He wanted to shut his mouth and walk away. But he couldn't hide from what he saw – not with this heart on his sleeve. It seemed to push him at the girl.

Instead of retreating, he sat down next to her.

"You want this back, don't you?" he said quietly. She shook her head again, but he pressed on. "Without it, you're just like I was, aren't you? You can't say anything, can't do anything – nobody sees you."

She looked at him with a funny expression. "Yes," she said, her voice trembling.

"I don't ever want to be like that again," Mark declared, thinking of all the times his face had reddened as he fled in angry impotence from the taunts and jeers of the other kids. Of all the times his parents had stood behind him nudging him forward, forcing him to stand in the middle of groups of people when he only wanted to run and hide. Of all the times he'd heard adults say things that he *knew* were just flat wrong, but his mouth had remained locked shut.

And then he smiled as a possibility came to him. It risked everything he'd gained in these short twenty-four hours, but if it worked…

"Maybe… Maybe we could share it," he suggested.

Tricia looked puzzled. Mark slid closer to her on the bench, and then closer still, until their arms touched.

Her eyes widened and she moved away. She huddled in the corner like a trapped possum, pinned in by the armrest at the end of the bench.

"What?" she whispered.

And then Mark mushed his shoulder against hers, and she felt a familiar tug on her arm. Fingers of warmth and energy flowed into her, spreading through her body. She had felt dead, empty. Now she felt alive again. The scared lines vanished from her face and were replaced by a sparkle in her eye. Tricia felt her tongue loosen, her limbs lighten.

With the joy came a shadow of compassion; she didn't want to sentence this boy to live in the deadly-quiet pit forever.

She saw his face darken, his lips clench, as the heart began tearing away from his arm. She realized what taking back her heart would mean to the boy. She couldn't do this to him... not even if it meant her own imprisonment. She placed her hand on his skinny chest, closed her eyes and shoved.

* * * * *

When he pushed his shoulder against hers, Mark felt the vibrance and energy draining from his arm. Suddenly, he was afraid.

He didn't want to give up the heart; he didn't want to be the cowed, quiet loser that everyone ignored, a boy trapped within himself.

He desperately wanted to pull free of the girl, keep the heart to himself. But he reminded himself that the heart was hers, and if it wanted to go back to her, then he couldn't keep it prisoner on his own arm. He understood the feeling of being trapped too well, and he saw in her face that the heart was even now keying open Tricia's inner lock.

Mark felt his tongue tightening and inwardly cried, *"No, don't take away my voice again!"*

Then Tricia's hand was on his body, pushing him backwards, separating their heart-joined arms. With a rush of indrawn air, he felt their connection cut, and the playground spun dizzily before his eyes. He blinked, twice, trying to slow the divebomb attack on his senses.

Mark shook his head to clear the cobwebs and saw Tricia doing the same.

At the same moment, eyes wide, mouths open in surprise, each raised a finger to point at the other's arm.

There, above each of their elbows, throbbing contentedly, perched a glowing, red, beating heart. They were smaller by far than the single heart the boy and girl had passed between them, but that didn't matter.

Mark felt his tongue was tighter perhaps than it had been an hour ago, but certainly more free than before he had taken the quivering heart Tricia had offered him yesterday.

Tricia was smiling. Reaching slowly across Mark's lap, she took his hand. The heart on his arm beat faster. Hers quickened visibly in response.

"Maybe I won't get in so much trouble now that it's smaller," she mused.

"Maybe they'll grow," he answered, and they stood.

Hand in hand, neither yelling nor sulking, they answered the bell signalling the end of recess.

Frost

When the fog turned to frost, David's life, for an eternal second, froze. And then, like an icicle slapped from a gutter to smash onto the whitened asphalt below, David's life fractured. And reformed in a forever altered pattern.

* * * * *

"Look, Dad," David tugged at his father's shirtsleeve. "There are snowflakes on the plane window!"

Merle Currier nodded with disinterest at his son's discovery of the physical effects of altitude.

"It's just the humidity on the window that's turning to ice," he mumbled, eyes barely leaving his paper. "When we left Dallas, it was hot and muggy. It's freezing in Minneapolis, so we must be getting close."

David looked up at his father with a less-than-appreciative eye. "Looks like snowflakes," he grumbled.

Merle didn't answer, but instead turned to the next page of the *Wall Street Journal.*

David began to hum. Tunelessly. In just the way that he knew would get a reaction. It didn't take long.

A large paw released the edge of the newspaper for a moment and cuffed the boy firmly on the head.

"Cool it, David," his father growled.

The boy huffed to himself. The whole trip had been like this. For brief moments, his father would condescend to stoop to David's eight-year-old level and play. But then just as quickly, the older man would disappear into the reams of newsprint that seemed to carpet his bachelor's apartment, or pick up the phone and speak in clipped, hushed terms to whoever was on the other end. And David was expected to sit still on the couch and watch TV. And not make any noise. Or he'd be going to bed early.

David went to bed early *a lot*.

Last night was a good case in point. After a quiet (boring) dinner of warm-it-up-in-the-oven-from-a-box chicken and canned beans, father and son had moved into the living room. David toyed with his TW-4 truck, revving and crashing the silver and blue metal cab into the base of the television stand. It made a satisfying thud.

"Cool it, David," came the gruff rebuke from the couch. So he had. His dad was watching some tedious TV show with a group of old men sitting around a table. They talked about things like "stock growth" and "strategic ventures" and "capital," though they didn't say of what state. David grabbed for the channel changer.

"Don't touch that, David," his father had warned.

But he had touched it.

He picked it up and methodically punched every button that he could.

Twice.

His dad didn't even yell that loud. One big, hairy hand grabbed David's own and relieved him of the remote control. The other heaved him up by his pants and levitated him straight to bed.

David didn't like visiting his father much.

Then again, he couldn't say that living with Mom was any picnic either. She was always yelling at him, and sending him to his room.

Just before coming on this trip, she'd been sitting at their kitchen table, smoking a cigarette and talking and laughing on the phone with her friend Rachel. She had been promising all day to play Nintendo with him, and instead she was on the phone for an hour! He had given up on the video game, and started idly punching around a beach ball he'd dug out of the hall toy closet. When it bounced over the kitchen chair and knocked Mom's can of Coke into her lap, she'd stopped laughing. She hissed something into the phone, set it to the side and said the two words he had come to know so well: "You're grounded!"

When she'd brought him to the airport and left him with the stewardess to chaperone on the plane flight to his Dad's, he thought she looked relieved to see him go.

If he could, he'd divorce the both of them himself. He'd heard of a kid doing that somewhere, but he had no idea how. Lawyers'd cost a lot of money, he figured. Way more than the $3.82 he had in his pocket. He pushed his hand in there and felt the change, warm and slippery against his hip. He stole a glimpse at his dad, who seemed to have hair in all the wrong places. It stole out and over the elastic collar of his Vikings sweatshirt, snuck through the pleats in his gold watchband, and even peeked out of the sides of his ears. Dad had tiny hairs poking through the holes in his wide-pored and pudgy nose, and a couple of stray silver hairs strained above his thickened eyebrows. But above those eyebrows rose the creeping lines of bare flesh. If you looked at the top of Dad's head, you could see right through the hair to the scalp beneath. David felt a rush of disgust overcome him, and turned back to the window. Dad was gross!

The frost on the window had lengthened since just moments before. An intricate webwork of crystal and lace traced patterns of winter across the inner glass of the double-paned — but somehow still flimsy-looking — airplane window. David stared at the filigree, following its paths and crosscuts, marvelling at its delicate beauty. He raised a finger to the window, tracing the currents in the pane of snow. But as his finger touched the window, the frost on the other side of the glass jumped.

"Hey, watch it!" a tiny voice bellowed.

The frost beneath the pad of his index finger suddenly swirled, twined and coalesced. And just above his finger, a small figure grew. It was white, but with glints of red and blue and green. It looked like a man, but a tiny one. *Really* tiny. Not more than an inch tall.

David yanked his finger away from the glass.

"Hey, who are you?" the boy asked. His voice trembled a little as he spoke.

From behind the rustle of the newspaper his father shushed him. "Who're you talking to, Davy? Keep it down. People are sleeping."

David repeated his question in a whisper. "Who are you?"

"They call me Kyla Kulmavoetud."

"What kinda name is that?" David asked.

The tiny creature grinned. His teeth were crystal sharp, his eyes flashed the blue of frozen air. David could almost see right through him.

"It's a name that says what I am — icy, numb, cold as snow. I'm a frost sprite."

The sharp-looking creature waited a beat for the import to sink in.

"Having a nice flight?" the sprite asked. Its tone didn't sound as friendly as its words.

David wasn't sure if he wanted to answer. Did the "don't talk to strangers" rule apply to inch-tall frost sprites? So he shrugged.

"Not getting on with the old man, eh?"

David shrugged again, but this time a pair of tears instantly brimmed in his eyes.

"You don't talk much, do ya, kid?"

David rubbed his eyes quickly, then leaned forward towards the window. In a low whisper, he asked, "Can you do magic? Will you give me three wishes, like Aladdin?"

"Do I look like a genie, kid?" The sprite gestured at his miniscule, nearly transparent waist. "Ice and snow. The size of a quarter and not half as hard."

The boy's expectant expression fell.

"A frost sprite can't change the world," Kyla said. Then winked. "But we can change how it looks. Shall I show you the treachery of clouds? Maybe make you the dance partner of a dragon?"

David drew back a bit. Shook his head. "I'd fall!"

"Qui-etttttttt," his father growled again.

"I'll fall," David whispered to the sprite.

"So what if you do? Anyway, you won't if you're with me."

"Like Superman when he took Lois Lane...?"

The sprite arched an eyebrow of ice, then reached through the glass. "Take my hand."

David looked at the ghostly palm extended towards him. "I'll crush it!"

"Take it."

David glanced at his father, and then at the passengers around them. Nobody seemed to be paying him and his conversation any attention. Shrugging to himself — what did he have to lose? — he touched a finger to the sprite's magical palm...

...and was suddenly standing outside the airplane! And he was tiny! The sprite's crystalline hand fit snugly in his own, and the window where he'd just been looking out seemed as tall now as the Sears Tower. He squinted, trying to see back in through the window, but the interior of the plane was a shadowy world of black and grey compared to the sparkle and glint of the white ice and smoky air that floated all around them.

"Come on," exclaimed the sprite and with a quick crouch-turned-leap, yanked David off the wing of the plane and out into a haze of chilling snow.

"Yeeeeoooooaaaaaaahhh!!!" screamed the boy as they fell through a whirlwind of clouds. The air was cool, but not too cold on David's neck. He finally stopped his screaming and realized that, while they were in the middle of the sky without a parachute, they weren't actually *falling*. He took a deep breath; it tasted full and sharp and sweet, not claustrophobic and sour, like the air he'd tasted for the past week. He giggled suddenly and extended his arms to fly. He was free! David howled again, this time with delight. The sprite only nodded, his icy teeth glinting in the sun.

What would Dad say if he could see me now? David thought, and then looked back to see the plane. Already it was disappearing in the rolling heavy cushion of cloud. His elation vanished as quickly as it had come. His heart trembled with panic. How would they get back? The plane was moving *fast!*

"Wait," he cried out. Flipping away from Kyla, he began to dogpaddle his way toward the plane. He struck out with his hands and feet, kicking the way they'd taught him at the community pool. The cotton yielded easily at his clawing arms and pounding feet, but it didn't feel as if he was moving forward. The cloud wasn't thick enough for his hands to really *push* against anything to move himself forward.

Behind him he heard the frost sprite laugh.

He kicked hard and struck out with his hands cupped, but they only came back damp with moisture. It was as if he was waving his arms in the backyard, pretending he was a bird. He could wave them all he wanted, but he never left the ground.

A tear of frustration rolled down his cheek, and then something cold whooshed past his face. He couldn't see anymore! The world was a white blur of watery fluff. Not only was he not getting closer to the plane, he was not keeping his head above the clouds.

He was falling!

The white tendrils wound around his arms, covered his face. It was almost too thick to breathe. He gagged on its chewy, sno-cone wetness, choked on fear and fog. He opened his mouth to scream again, but found that he didn't have enough air in his lungs to make a sound.

Closing his eyes and balling his fists, David quit skyswimming, and really began to cry. It was a weak, defeated yowl. His tears were almost indistinguishable from the icy water that was streaking across his face, but cry he did. He curled into a ball and hugged his legs. He hated everyone. Everything. The world was too mean to him. So just let him drop like a rock to the ground. What did he care? At least he wouldn't have to sit in Dad's stuffy apartment anymore, or hear Mom yell and complain like Erkle, the Carrington's yappy schnauzer next door.

"It appears I have made a sorry mistake. The child is quite obviously a *chtschlept*. A wimpering chimp. A quitter."

The voice was close, almost in his ear. David opened his eyes to see Kyla floating along beside him, head on his hand, elbow pointed at the clouds beneath them. He looked as if he was lying on a living room floor watching TV.

David's eyes grew wide and his mouth began to open in a grin. But then he stopped himself, and stubbornly looked away. He'd had enough of frost sprites, too. He began to hum, louder and louder. As off-key and jarring as possible. He closed his eyes and hummed the sprite and the rest of the world away.

"Hmmm. Well, it's a long way down. Hours maybe. You don't fall very fast when you're this size. I think you'll come down somewhere near Chicago. If that's where you really want to go. I'll go part of the way with you, in case you change your mind."

David refused to meet the sprite's gaze. He was enjoying the black anger that had taken hold of him. *"Don't give him the satisfaction,"* is what his mom would say. And he didn't.

Except...

The sprite didn't say another word, and after a few minutes of quiet, David wondered if he was still there. He couldn't see anything — this was worse than being in the bathroom after taking a long, hot shower. He couldn't see a foot in front of him. Everything was white. And that was scarier than being in dark. But pulling his arms resolutely across his chest, David vowed not to turn his head. He would be scared *"like a man,"* as Dad was keen on telling him.

Then again, why would he want to do something that Dad told him to do?

Suddenly he broke through the ceiling of clouds, and David could see a lot farther than a foot in front of him. He could see for miles and miles and miles. And that was worse than everything being white or dark, because now he could see how high he was. How completely helpless. And he could hear the wind whistling in his ears as he plummeted through the open air. He was picking up speed.

"Ahhhhh!" he shrieked, and jerked his head around looking for the frost sprite.

Kyla was still lying in the air next to him, one arm supporting his head, his elbow resting on an invisible pillow of air.

"Can I be of some service?" the icy man grinned. David didn't think he sounded helpful at all. His voice was frigid. But who else could he turn to?

"Help!" David yelped.

"What would you like me to do?" Kyla asked, wickedly ignoring the boy's plight.

"Stop me from falling!"

Kyla tilted his head, glancing first at David, and then below, measuring the distance between the boy and ground. He looked bored. Finally, with a shrug, he extended his arm.

"Take my hand."

David snatched at the crystal man's frosty palm.

The whine of air in his ears abruptly quieted; David knew that the sprite had stopped their fall.

"How come you can fly and I can't?" he asked, after catching his breath.

The sprite stared without expression at David. His eyes were now black stones set in shards of glass.

"We do have *some* magic. Now, where would you like to go? To the top of a mountain? As far from your father and mother as possible, yes? To the North Pole?"

David shook his head. "No, it's cold there. How about someplace warm. Like Hawaii?"

The sprite threw his head back and laughed. "You'd be swimming right through me in about two minutes if we went to Hawaii. What do you think I'm made of, plastic?"

David's face fell. "You'd melt, huh?"

"Let's just say I wouldn't be very solid company."

The sprite put a finger to his forehead and tapped, once, twice, five times.

"Ever fly like a bird?"

"Not before today," David giggled.

The sprite gripped David's hand tighter and swooped down and to their left. David could see the geometric outlines of fields and subdivisions below, colored like a brown and white checkerboard quilt. Then, directly in front of them, he saw it.

Brown and black, with eyes of golden, untouchable fire. It looked as large as a plane, but its wings were flapping fast and hard, and no plane David had ever seen had wings that did that.

It was a robin, just like the kind that had divebombed his head last year in the backyard because he'd disturbed a nest of babies in the hedge. David fingered his forehead absently, where the mother robin had pecked a bloody, painful hole before he had managed to roll to the ground and escape.

They flew alongside the robin. Inches from that sharp, pale orange panting beak. Slowly its eyes swiveled to track them, never pausing an instant in its flight. David cringed, but the sprite laughed.

"You're only an inch tall once in your life, right? Live a little. Wouldn't you like to wrap your arms around that bird's neck and squeeze? Hard?"

David shook his head and the sprite laughed.

They moved in closer. The bird opened its beak to bite.

"Nooooo!" the boy shouted, as the yawning blackness of its maw stretched wide to descend on his head. But the clack of its beak closing came a second later from beneath them. Then they were astride the bird, grasping oily smooth feathers as the surprised creature swooped up, then dove down, trying to dislodge its unwanted passengers.

With a firm but reassuring grip, Kyla held David by the upper arm, pushing the boy's face down into the musty black fuzz of feathers at the angry bird's neck. The ground swam dizzily closer as the bird shrieked and flew madly at the earth.

"We're going to crash!" David cried.

"Hold on," the sprite whispered in his ear, and then he was gone.

David looked up and saw the sprite spark like a dart of light in front of the bird. The bird squealed and banked to the left, then cawed and swooped to the right. But no matter which direction it moved, the sprite was there, dancing an irritating, airy jig just out of reach of the bird's beak.

David could see a look of madness enter the bird's golden eyes. The kind of look a mouse made when it was caught in a trap behind mom's couch. David felt sorry for the mice, even though it was he who set the traps. Mom couldn't look at a dead mouse, she said, so he had to take care of the rodents. Otherwise they'd get in his Captain Crunch and he wouldn't have anything left for breakfast.

Finally, after what seemed like hours of frantic dodging and diving, he felt the bird's wings slow their frantic pace. They were really barely treading air when the frost sprite tapped a finger on the tip of the exhausted bird's beak and then flipped himself end over end to land astride its neck.

"So where do you want to go?" Kyla asked, and pulled sharply on a neck feather with his left hand. The bird flinched. David felt a shiver in the twisting spine beneath him, but the bird seemed to change its course accordingly.

"Dunno," the boy mumbled, thinking about the look in the bird's eye. He kept seeing the mice he killed, and feeling the bad pit in his stomach that he felt every time he emptied a trap. The same pit he felt when he entered his dad's apartment last weekend.

"Maybe we should let the bird go."

"After the trouble I just went through to tame him? I should say not. Now come on. What would you like to see? The top of a mountain? The Frost City of the clouds? An ice dragon?"

David considered for a moment. He wondered if his dad had even noticed his absence yet. Would he be worried about him? Or would he just go on reading his stupid paper? He shook a tear from his eye and blinked. He was free now. He could go wherever he wanted, and not have to worry about what Mom or Dad would say.

"Let's see them all!"

"Now you're talking, kid. But we'll need to change horses. This old bird will never make it to the top of a mountain. Ready?"

Before David could finish a shrug, the sprite had whisked them off the bird's back and high into the air. David felt a pang of relief as the bird shot away from them in the opposite direction, happy to be free of its passengers.

"Mountain first," the sprite announced, and David gripped Kyla's cold hand tighter in his own.

Time seemed to stretch shorter and wider as they swam through curls of cloud and bursts of blue sky. The sun melted to purple on the horizon, and then David saw the peak. It was *below* them!

Mt. Everest coming up."

David had fantasized before about climbing a mountain. In his dreams he was tall, strong and bronze, with muscles bulging from his arms and a steely, macho glint to his eye. He would hammer and pick his way up the cruel granite face, leading a band of other climbers up from below. When he reached the top, he'd plant a bright yellow flag and stand proudly surveying the world below him; he would be the tallest man on earth. When he pulled the other climbers up with a rope, they would thank him and tell him he was the best. The strongest mountain climber ever.

But when David and Kyla landed on the top of Mount Everest, there wasn't much about it that resembled his childish fantasy.

The mountain top was rocky and icy and not very pleasant at all. Nobody proclaimed him a hero. He didn't feel very strong, either. Heck, Kyla had to hold onto his arm to keep him from blowing away.

David's teeth chattered as the sprite led him along the spiky, slippery tip of the mountain. "Even I can't make you feel very warm up here," Kyla apologized. "Not enough air. Not enough magic. But look. You can see the sunset."

The sprite was right. David turned to the west to stare, as the solid orange globe of the sun crept closer and closer to the edge of the earth. The sky merged from red to purple to black above them as the dot of fire grew smaller, weaker, and then abruptly went out. It was the most beautiful thing he had ever seen, and he was the most uncomfortable he'd ever been.

"Sometimes you have to suffer a little for the reward," the sprite announced. "Had enough?"

David nodded quickly, and they were airborne again.

"Hidden in the Western Aerenvil Mists is the lair of an ice dragon," Kyla announced. "His name is Hrrrl and he's a very cross beast. They say his dreams are the source of nightmares to children all around the world. And those are his good dreams."

David's eyes grew wide as golfballs. "Is it safe to go near him?"

"You'll soon learn that nothing in life is safe, child. But you can approach any sort of beast with caution and, if you're lucky and brave, come away with all your limbs still attached."

"Why go near the beasts at all?"

The sprite laughed, his cackle the sound of ice breaking

and shattering.

"Why, indeed! Why have you come near me?"

"You're not a beast!"

"Aren't I?" The sprite grinned again, teeth glinting like daggers. David shivered.

"Know this, boy: approach any beast with a cool head and a brave heart and you will, at the very least, earn its respect, even if it still slays you. Try to avoid a beast and it will seek you out when you least expect it, and sink its fangs into your back before you even know it's there. It will toy with you and tease you, and mock you for your fear."

David thought about that for a moment, imagining himself spearing a snorting, howling, scaly dragon with the tip of the broom his mother kept behind the door in their utility room. He'd pretended in the past that the broom was a lance, and the pile of laundry a deadly dragon. But now that he was actually to meet up with a real dragon, and not a collection of smelly socks and shirts and underthings...

"But what if I'm not strong enough to beat the beast?" David asked. "Shouldn't I hide?"

"Strength comes from the heart, not the biceps, boy. You can beat any beast if you believe deeply. If you run away to hide all the time you're likely to become a beast yourself."

"How could I become a beast?" David asked. "I'm a kid!"

"Beasts aren't born as such," the sprite replied. "But as they grow, they hide and plot and fear. They stew poison and watch it curdle in hidden spaces. Their faces draw up grey and wrinkled. Sometimes they grow scales and fingernails the size of lawn darts. Sometimes they turn to ice. Whatever they grow into, they rarely like to face the light. And they rarely admit what they have become."

"Was Hrrrl a boy like me once?"

"Why don't you ask him? He's right over there."

Kyla pointed to their right, and David sucked in a sharp gasp. Towering above a mountainous cloud was the largest dragon he'd ever seen. Well, it was the *only* dragon he'd ever seen, but it was truly monstrous. It was a jeweled beast, geometric scales of ice stretching from haunches to head in a blinding prism of violet and electric blue and emerald. But mostly, Hrrrl was ice white. And his eyes, which looked larger than David's whole body, flashed from crimson to black as the dragon became aware of its visitors.

Hrrrl's legs and tail disappeared into a dense canopy of fog, but there was no mistaking the beast's intentions. Its forelegs stretched, and twin iridescent wings unfurled from its sides like gargantuan kites. The dragon was readying itself to pounce.

"He's going to kill us!" David shrieked.

The beast's mouth opened, and from it issued the loudest, most terrifying sound David had ever heard. It was louder than the engines of a jet taking off, more tortured than the wail of train brakes when the engineer sees a car blocking the tracks just a couple hundred yards ahead. With the sound came a blast of arctic cold that washed over David and Kyla like a tidal wave.

David felt his eyelashes turn to ice.

"Ask him." Kyla said again. He squeezed David's hand.

"I can't," the boy cried. "He's going to eat us!"

Without so much as a "See ya," the sprite vanished. The dragon roared again, this time taking two steps through the clouds so that his monstrous snout leveled with the boy's eyes. David could have reached out and touched the beast's frozen teeth. They spiked up and down in its mouth like the icicles hanging off Mom's gutters at home. He floundered in the air, waving his arms like a drowning infant. In terror he looked up and down and around for the sprite, and called out the little man's name.

"Kyla! Kyla, help!"

Then he thought, *I'll fall. And if I fall, I'll get away from the dragon. Then I'll be safe for awhile.*

But David stared into the burning blue eyes of Hrrrl and

knew that he wasn't going to fall this time. He could not run away. For a second, he wondered if his own eyes mirrored those of a trapped mouse. Or the bird.

In his head, he heard Kyla's earlier admonitions. *"Strength comes from the heart. You can beat any beast if you believe."* And, *"Ask him."*

In front of him, the stakes of ice gleamed, slowly drawing apart. Hrrrl was preparing to eat him. David shrugged his shoulders, *What have I got to lose?*

"Were you ever a boy like me?" David said, his voice a tremulous whisper.

The dragon dipped its head, raising a frosted brow. "Eh?" it growled.

David repeated his question. Louder this time. "I said, were you ever a boy, like me?"

Hrrrl didn't move. Didn't answer. One eyelid closed. Then the other.

David didn't know what to think. Had the dragon just gone to sleep? If it had, maybe he could try to escape...

...No. He had asked a question, and he wanted an answer. There was no outracing a dragon in its own cloud. Heck, he couldn't even keep himself aloft without the help of the frost sprite. Although he seemed to be holding his own now.

"Hrrrl," he said, raising his voice another level. "I asked if you were ever a boy. A human boy."

"Yeeessss," the beast hissed, its eyes springing open. The force of its breath knocked David backwards. He tumbled through the moist fog, coming to rest many yards away from the icy beast.

"I was a boy. I had parents, just like you," the dragon growled. "But I hated them. I hated everybody. But that's all over now. Because now I'm the most powerful beast in the world!!!"

David thought for a moment. "But you're up here in the clouds, all by yourself."

"I LIKE to be alone." the dragon bellowed, fountains of fog steaming through his craterlike nostrils.

"Aren't you lonely?"

"Leave me alone!" the dragon turned tail and dove deep into a veil of cloud.

"Not bad," a voice chimed in his ear. "I told you, be brave and face your foes. Even if you don't have a broom."

"How do you know about the broom?" David asked, turning to see the frost sprite. Kyla lounged in the air beside him, legs crossed, head resting on his hand. He looked like a frozen genie.

"I know a lot of things about you," the sprite said. "Why do you think I chose *you* to take from the plane and not another kid?"

David shrugged.

"How about a stop in Halla, the Frost City?"

"Can I get a drink there?" David asked.

"You can get whatever you want there," the sprite replied, "as long as it's made of water. And it's cold." With a whoosh of speed, they left the cloud of the dragon behind.

It was beautiful! Sweeping spires of intricately molded ice rose from turrets of fog and snow to make a fairyland scene. The streets were endless, and wreathed in flowing cotton. The sprite held David's hand as they walked along a path through swirls of cloud dust closer and closer to the peaks of the city. There was music in the air, a high, pure, angelic wash of sound that made David's heart leap. It was cool and perfect, and utterly devoid of the aching passions of pain and love. Suddenly he yearned to be inside the twin towers of ice that marked the city's entrance. He wanted to stay here, to be a human boy living in a castle in the clouds. His life would be a fairytale. People would write about him, the boy in the sky.

Kyla nodded at the keepers of the gate, twin wraiths of many arms, eyes and motions. They shimmied away from the opening, allowing the boy and sprite passage into the

126

city. As they passed through the gate, David saw a wondrous mix of beings dancing through a crystalline square. Winged creatures fluttered delicately above, while many-legged white beetles skated dizzily across the open ground. The song floated in the air. Frost sprites dashed between doorways, and snowy hummingbirds feasted at frozen nectar in a garden of glass.

They passed through a door, and walked quickly down a blinding hallway.

"You'll stay here," Kyla said, escorting David into a small room. A cot was set up in one corner, across from a window that looked onto the square they'd just crossed.

"I'll be back for you at breakfast. Sleep tight." And with a wink, the sprite was gone.

David stared out onto the frozen square, watched as cool white lights flickered on in windows across the way. Slowly, the skaters and flyers disappeared and the fairy garden was left still; an ice sculpture hidden in a cloud.

Sighing, David climbed into the cot. Ice crystals crunched beneath him as he shifted in the bed. The heavy sheets did nothing to warm him, and he couldn't find a comfortable way to rest his head. He missed his own pillow. His own bed. Even the bed at Dad's! Idly he wondered if sprites from this city ever left to try to make it on their own in a human town.

The night passed slowly. David felt the cold creeping through his fingers and toes. But it wasn't coming from Halla, or even the frozen bed. The cold was steaming out of his heart. He felt it knotting up like a fat icicle inside as he reminded himself of the dull weeks he spent with his father and the heated flashes of temper that drove him to wish for escape from his mother. Wasn't it better to stay here and hug the ice to his chest? To become a frost sprite himself, maybe?

He lay still in the bed of ice and pictured the frost covering him completely. He felt his lips turning blue and his cooling blood flowed ever more sluggishly.

Sometime during the night, he thought his heart stopped.

Kyla picked him up the next morning.

"What's for breakfast?" David asked, stuffing a fist into his mouth to stifle a yawn.

"Slept well, did you?" the sprite asked.

"Not really."

"Hmmm." The sprite looked grim for a moment, then dropped its eyes to the ground.

"There are two menus to choose from," Kyla said. "But whichever one you choose is the one you must live on for the rest of your life. After this meal, there is no going back. Follow me."

They walked through a maze of icy corridors. Tiny gauzy fairies zipped out of their way, while snow beetles sunk like water through the floor to avoid their steps. At last they stepped into a huge open room.

Twisting spires of ice rose from the floor, glittering with a faint rainbow tinge all across the room. At each stalagmite, a transparent creature, or two or three, fed, licking greedily at the delicate spikes of ice.

"If you choose the ice, you will stay here in the clouds," Kyla said. His eyes were dead stones. "Forever."

The sprite looked at David with its frighteningly still gaze.

"In the clouds you will not feel the pain. Your heart won't ever feel like it's being sliced in two by an electric knife. But the ice doesn't taste anything like a hot stack of pancakes dripping with maple syrup. It tastes like ice. It will leave you numb, kyla."

"Your name means numb?"

The sprite nodded grimly. "You will sing and fly and dance… but you will not really *feel*. You won't get that pit in your stomach that you get when you visit your father, but you won't feel that hot maple syrup feeling that you get when he tells you he's proud to be your dad, either."

David thought for a moment, watching the crystalline creatures of the cloud flit and flutter.

A distant chime sounded like a tinkle of tiny bells. The whole scene looked so fragile, he felt as if he could shatter it with a sneeze.

"You must choose."

"If I stayed, it wouldn't be very brave, would it?" David asked.

Kyla shook his head. "Not if you stay only because you are running away from your parents. From your fear. From the possibility of pain."

"But I can beat any beast if I try, right? If I'm really brave?"

"There's a good chance, yes."

"Then I'll choose…"

David looked longingly at the scene around him. Thought of shivering on a mountain top while seeing the most beautiful sunset in the world; thought of feeling afraid, but still beating a dragon with a simple question. Thought of Dad's apartment and Mom's mousetraps.

"…pancakes."

* * * * *

David ran ahead of his father down the narrow hallway and into the airport waiting area. The sprite had dropped him back in his seat just before landing. Dad didn't seem to have noticed that he'd been gone.

"Be brave," the icy creature had said, and then David was staring at a window of intricate frost lacery. Try as he might, he couldn't locate anything in the crystal pattern that looked remotely like the tiny man. The page of a newspaper crinkled familiarly next to him, as his dad folded up the *Wall Street Journal* into a neat, complete stack.

After awhile, David began to hum. Not the cool beauty

129

of the Frost City square song, but the friendly tones of his father's Simon & Garfunkel records and his mother's Barry Manilow tapes. His fingers and toes warmed to the glow of the songs of home. And Dad didn't tell him, "Cool it."

"David, over here," his mother called. The boy ran to her and hugged her tight.

"Was he good for you, Merle?" she asked when his father came up from behind. David could hear the brakes she put on her voice whenever she talked to his father.

"Good as gumdrops," Dad growled, ruffling David's hair with a hand.

"Did you have a good flight?"

"Not bad. Kinda cold on the plane, I thought."

His mother felt David's hands to see. "Did you get cold, kiddo?"

"I'm fine," he said, pulling his hands back. "It wasn't that cold."

"How about I buy us all breakfast before I head to the hotel?" Dad volunteered. "The food on the plane was…" he wrinkled his mouth in disgust, "…plane food."

His mother didn't answer right away, her face wrinkling as if to sneeze… or complain. But then David could see her expression shift.

"Okay. But then we've got to get going."

* * * * *

They all sat down at a noisy IHOP near the airport. There was music playing on the radio with bells and strings and guitars, and David thought it sounded somehow… *dirtier* than the music of the clouds. Certainly not angelic. And yet, he liked it better.

The waitress set a plate of steaming pancakes in front of him, along with a rack of flavored syrups.

His parents looked at each other with tight mouths, but then smiled as they watched David dig into the food.

It warmed his stomach like a big, bright fire. He mixed the syrups indiscriminately, pouring boysenberry, strawberry and maple syrup all over the cakes while his parents beamed.

"Merry Christmas, son," his dad said.

His mom sighed and then nodded her head. "Yes, Merry Christmas."

In his heart, David felt a rime of frost melt away.

Anne's Perfect Smile

The Post-it hadn't been there long.

Every night since Anne's disappearance I'd kept vigil before this framed photo of her. Long silken hair of moonlight and shadow, eyes crisp in a silent smile, teeth gleaming straight and white against lips pursed to say, "Darling, I love you."

And this morning, when I woke, there was a Post-it stamped crookedly across that smile.

Written in her loopy hearts and hugs script it read, "Tonight, if you would see me one last time, come to 139 Rue de Mort at 10 p.m."

She had been here! Why hadn't she woken me? Why this cloak and dagger game? It occurred to me that the note and its "one last time" meant perhaps she had not been kidnapped, as I had suggested to the police.

Maybe she had left me of her own accord, to live with another man. Or joined a cult? She'd always had an untoward fascination with the dark side. Our bookshelves were lined with the evidence.

I paced the house, trying to understand. Reread the Post-it again and again. What if *she* hadn't delivered the note? That thought chilled some of the tears from my eyes. Could some thug have been in my bedroom last night? I dismissed the idea quickly. If this was a kidnapper's scheme, what was the ransom? The note had asked for nothing.

Rue de Mort was a tiny street on the outskirts of town near the acreage of St. Mary Cemetery. I'd never been in this particular area before, it didn't look inviting. The handful of houses were rotting and dark; I suspected most to be uninhabited.

There was no light on in the house, but I climbed the creaking wooden steps anyway and knocked. The door fell open at my touch.

"Anne?" I called inside.

There was a thump, and then I heard her voice for the first time in weeks.

"In here," she called. Two simple words, but my heart leapt with relief. She was all right!

I stepped into the blue-black shadows of the house, and strained my eyes to see into the room. A flame erupted from the oily black and there was Anne, a candle in hand, moving toward me.

Her face seemed pale in the orange glow of the flame, but there was no mistaking the perfect gleam of her smile. She was happy to see me.

"Come into the living room," she said, and gestured to a couch I could barely make out in the gloom.

"What's going on?" I asked. "Why don't you have any lights on?"

And then I saw him.

Silent and thin, he watched from a sheet-covered chair. His eyes glinted dangerously.

"And who is he?" I pointed.

"Sit." She pushed me down on the couch.

"What's going on is, this is my new home, I prefer the dark, and he is my new husband, Derrick. I wanted you to have the chance to meet him. Derrick, say hello."

The strangely-still form sitting across from me whispered a steely greeting. "Welcome to our home," he said. His too-wide smile lacked any warmth.

"But you can't have another husband," I yelled, getting angrier by the instant. "We haven't gotten divorced! You're *my* wife!"

"I *was* your wife," she corrected. "The vows said, 'til death do you part.'"

"But neither of us are dead," I sputtered, suddenly realizing that perhaps I should be scoping the room for an escape route.

It was then that I noticed the coffin.

"Jack, *I'm* dead."

I laughed nervously at that. "And I suppose that coffin is where you sleep at night."

"Don't be silly," she replied. "Those stories are romantic, but *dead* wrong. The coffin is for you."

I launched myself from the couch then, but I'd waited too long. I never saw him leave the chair, but Derrick had me restrained in seconds. The intimacy of his embrace allowed me an all-too-close whiff of his hygiene.

"At least I always knew when to shower," I said.

"Wouldn't do any good, dear," my apparently ex-wife sighed. "The dead simply stink. But they do eat well. And I've had a craving for you since I died."

Anne opened her mouth then, revealing horribly extended canines. As her lips touched my neck for the last time in my life, it occurred to me that all the money I'd spent to have her teeth capped had been wasted.

A Lack of Signs

T here was no sign in the window. No hours posted on the door. Only the beckoning chill of the pink neon tube that ringed the shuttered window and the cool iceberg blue of its brother that outlined the door.

Jan had passed the shop for weeks in her car, glancing to the north side of the street as the dead grass of the parkway skimmed by, a Banana Republic blur of bleak earthtone colors, wondering what was inside. The neon always seemed lit, but there was rarely a car in the lot. Now and then, she would drive by and notice people entering the tattoo parlor to the east of the unmarked shop, but there was never any traffic in the other half of the decaying strip mall. Just the call of the neon.

A call promising… what?

It had been a long day, but Jan didn't feel much like going home, not yet. There, she would only have to face the lonely chore of microwaving something to eat, while watching whatever mindless sitcom was on, to kill the hours and fill the void of silence until sleep rescued her briefly, before shitting her out into another day.

Tonight, would the studio audience exaggerate its excitement over an episode about the neighbor's boy cheating in grammar school and the kooky hijinks as his friends sought to save him from both his teacher and moral bankruptcy? Or would they take on an even more serious subject in a "very special episode" about drug or alcohol abuse? The lives portrayed in those shallow sitcoms often seemed more interesting than hers. While their problems often seemed ludicrous, at least they were *connected* to other people.

As she pulled away from the light at Glen Ellyn Road, she decided that now was as good a time as any. She was tired of being curious. Slapping on her turn signal, Jan crossed lanes and pulled into the parking lot of the name-less store. She sat still for a moment, staring at the blank, white-coated cinderblock exterior, then finally shut off the engine.

The store revealed no more clues as to its specialty from up close than it did from the road. There was clearly a light on inside, showing through the white shutters. And the neon glowed brightly. But cold. Neon never evoked warmth.

She could see the building itself was in disrepair, chunks of mortar missing from between blocks, peels of dirty white paint lifting from the windows and gutters and revealing slashes of black building bone beneath.

The parking lot only held two cars besides her own, a rusting Chevy Impala, and a beaten up black hot rod, she thought it was a Mustang.

Jeremy would have known for sure.

A bell jingled to announce her as the door shut the out-side out, quick as a guillotine. She knew immediately she had made a mistake.

The room was painted a chalky white, and carpeted in a neutral beige. The paint and carpet were new, but they had as much color and life as her apartment. It was like stepping into an eggshell that held no embryo.

The room was empty.

A lone bulb hung from the ceiling to light the room. A hallway led away into shadow. Jan shook her head at her own foolishness. There was no sign here because there was no business here. At least not yet.

Someone was probably redressing the space, and just taking awhile to do it. Maybe the new renters had run out of funds, and had had to postpone the opening of their new store, whatever it was to be. In any event, it did not appear to be a proprietorship of anything right now.

As Jan turned to leave, a voice reached out from the hallway.

"Can I help you?"

She peered back over her shoulder, keeping her hand on the handle of the glass door.

"I'm sorry," she said. "I didn't realize you weren't open yet."

"We're open," the voice answered, and Jan saw a face swim out of the darkness. He was an aged man, face warted and wrinkled like an old toad, but his eyes were gemstone blue and gleamed in the light from the unshielded bulb.

"What exactly is it that you're looking for?" he asked softly, his voice as soothing as his eyes were bright.

"I... I don't know," Jan said. She turned to the door and pushed, jangling the bell again. "I'll come back another time, when you have your displays set up."

"Come back soon," the old man answered, as she slipped back out to the parking lot. "Come back when you know what you want."

* * * * *

Jan's heart was still beating hard when she pulled into the potholed lot of her apartment complex, just a couple miles from the strange store. Something about the place, something about its cool interior, its wrinkled proprietor, its... emptiness, bothered her. Scared her, really.

When she'd stepped inside the store, she'd immediately felt disoriented, as if she were slipping... and then an overwhelming urge to run.

"What must he have thought of me," she said, shaking her head as she keyed open the apartment door. "Foolish woman, doesn't know what she wants..."

Jan set her things down on the small, white-tiled kitchen table, and took a breath. She had what she wanted. Her place, her stuff, her freedom.

She nodded at the matted posters so recently framed and hung. Street scenes of her favorite cities: Chicago's Michigan Avenue at night, New York 's Times Square at noon. The streets were filled with people in white pants and dark coats and electric pink midriffs and heads boasting warring baseball caps (*Cubs, White Sox, Orioles*), a quiet competition of sports franchises. The people walked across the sterile white of her walls, offering a glimpse of energy — of living.

Jan's life these days was all about filling space. Ever since Jeremy left and took with him all of the furniture in her heart. Not to mention her favorite blue ottoman. And the stereo system (*his since college*). And the DVD player (*you never watch movies*). She had signed the lease on this apartment the day after his brutal announcement (*you just don't move me anymore, I'm sorry*) and arrived the following weekend with a carload of clothes, dishes and old cassette tapes.

And the posters she'd reluctantly packed into peeling tubes when she'd first moved in with Jeremy the year before. He didn't like the city. *Too many people*, he said.

"You wanna move to Idaho and be a hermit?" she'd asked once. "Yeah, why not," he'd said. "At least the dumb-shit-per-capita is way down. And you can always get fresh potatoes." He'd laughed, and gone back to running down computer-simulated pedestrians with the help of his joystick and an IBM Pentium.

Eventually, he'd run her down as well. Run her down, then left her. Jan had still harbored hope that they could be together again, but then she'd gotten the call. He'd been run down too, by a green four-door sedan. But Jeremy's death had been no computer simulation. All she was left with were the pictures of their aborted life together. And the aching wish that she could have fulfilled his dream. She hadn't even gotten the chance to kiss him one last goodbye. The family had decided on a closed casket, and she'd been denied even that last bitter consolation.

Jan pulled a frozen carton of Swedish meatballs from the freezer and popped open the microwave door with a button. Five minutes. Enough to change and sort the mail, she thought, as the machine began to hum behind her.

But when she crossed the living room and saw the white, empty wall of the entryway again, she stopped. A trembling began in her calves and shivered its way through her thighs through her groin and belly, to lodge like a spear in the center of her chest. Jan drew a halting, pained breath, and without warning, began to sob.

She didn't hear the microwave's dinging reminders, five minutes later, from her fetal crouch on the perfect, unstained carpet.

* * * * *

"...if we could bump up the revenue projections on the transitional quotas, we could bury the loss margin on the Tablet software, right?"

Jan blinked, and looked up at Evie, her workmate who'd apparently been leaning, palms flat on her desk for the past couple minutes, going on about sales reports and who knew what else.

"Jan?"

"I'm sorry," she said. "I lost you there for a minute. What about the Tablet software?"

She'd been thinking about her living room, the way everything was so sterile, even with her street scene posters. Thinking about what she could fill the white space with. She couldn't paint, it wasn't hers to paint. But maybe an Oriental rug, with intricate twisting patterns of filigree and rich royal colors. Patterns to follow for hours with the eye, as the evenings slipped by...

Evie asked her question again, and managed, in the asking, to assign Jan with another job to do before day's end (*do you think you could help me and...*) and then she was gone, probably to kill the afternoon talking with her boyfriend on the phone. And Jan was left with more work and a burning question.

Would a blue rug work better in that space, or a burgundy?

* * * * *

Jeremy.

Her eyes welled up at the very thought of his name, and Jan suddenly couldn't see in the rush of traffic. Her chest was shuddering with sobs, and she pulled over into the first parking lot she came to. Shutting off the car, she buried her face in her hands and rested her forehead on the steering wheel.

It had been a few days, since she'd had an attack like this, and she cursed herself silently for it. Her lips murmured his name, over and over again as the tears flowed through the spaces between her fingers, and wet the wheel with her sorrow.

"*I want a family,*" he'd said.

"We could adopt," she'd begged.

"*I want my own family,*" he'd answered, and was gone.

Jan dried her eyes with a tissue from the glove box and shook the thoughts away. That was past. Jeremy was past. Her life was hers to do with as she chose.

And she chose to find an Oriental rug.

Sniffling a bit, she peered though the windshield to see where she was. In front of her, the cool glow of pink and blue neon shimmered and flickered. There was no sign in the shuttered window, but she knew immediately where she'd ended up.

Jan bit her lip, and focused on the idea of a vibrant, warm rug accenting the flat color of her apartment. The overpowering memory of Jeremy lessened.

She pulled the store's door open and stepped inside. Again the frame snapped shut with a crack and a jingle of bells. For a moment, just the briefest second, she felt disoriented and the edge of her vision seemed to swim with white and mauve and burgundy and blue.

Jan grasped at the door frame but then everything seemed to still, the colors slipping like sand into solid swaths of black, powder blue and royal purple.

The store felt much smaller than it had on her first visit, now it was full to bursting. The walls were hidden behind ornate tapestries, from the Middle East, tasseled and the dyed in rich hues. They were just mottled enough to make it certain that these were not mass produced, but handcrafted by artisans.

On the floor lined all about the shop were baskets and urns, woven in a tight knot of strawlike wicker, and varnished in varying shades of henna, oak and pale sand.

A cash register hid among a melange of pottery and bronzed vases atop a small display case where ornamental statues of elephants, rhinos and giraffes stalked within. There were beads hiding the hallway to the back recesses of the shop, and tall vertical stands that reached nearly to the ceiling, spaced evenly throughout the room. The stands were layered dozens deep in just what Jan had been looking for: Oriental carpets.

"So, you've decided what you want, have you?"

The voice came from behind the beads, which parted then and the old man passed through, a smile wide and bright wrinkling his cheeks.

"This is wonderful," Jan said, swiveling from side to side to take in the old man's stock. "I just decided today to find myself an Oriental rug. And these..." she gestured toward the rugs embroidered with deep reds and greens and blues and golds, "...are beautiful. You really should put up a sign, though. I would never have known this was here except..."

The old man's chill eyes twinkled, and he simply nodded.

She frowned then, and stepped over to view first one rug, and then the next, trying to surreptitiously find a price tag. The old man didn't move, just stood in the doorway before the beads.

"What do the prices on these range?" she finally asked.

He shrugged. "They are reasonable. We can discuss. But first," he nodded to the displays, "look. Look for your heart's desire."

With that, he vanished back from where he'd come, leaving Jan alone in the room. She ran her hands over the velvety fabric, admiring twists and twirls of satiny purple spiced with tangerine, and mauve laced with silver. *They were all beautiful,* she thought, turning from one pattern to the next, but always looking for the next, and the next, and the one that might be just a little better. More perfect. More her.

Finally, in the back of the store, just to the right of a clay pot hoarding a spray of fake flowers, she found it. A white tasseled rug with deep, rich blue runes, veined with burgundy streams and silver accents. Some of the twisting patterns doubled back on themselves like intricate knots. Others followed twining threads deeper and deeper into the pattern until they were lost, like creeks run down to their muddy grass-choked end.

"Yesss," Jan murmured, and jumped when a voice answered her.

"That'd be the one, eh?"

"Yes," she said, nodding exuberantly but then stilling her chin, slowing her enthusiasm, thinking of the rent that would be due soon, the rent that still didn't feel comfortable. She still worried that she wouldn't have enough in the bank to cover it, though so far she always had.

"How much?" she asked finally. The shopkeeper laughed.

"I can tell that this is the one for you, and I want to make sure you have it," he said. "In a regular store, this would go for upwards of a thousand dollars."

Jan could feel the blood drain from her face and her stomach twist.

"But I certainly didn't pay that much for it, and I know that you probably can't either. So let's find a solution that benefits us both. You get the rug you want, and I clear some space in my store and put some change in the cash drawer. How does $99 sound?"

Jan couldn't stop her lips from rising. It was more than she should spend, but she knew sh couldn't get a fake one for that price.

"I'll take it," she said.

The old man nodded, as if he'd expected nothing different. He lifted the rug from its hooks.

She'd worry about how she was going to pay for it later.

Jan shimmied the coffee table back and forth across the center of the Oriental rug. No matter how she positioned it, she couldn't seem to get it quite right.

Finally, she hit on lining up the edge of the table with the square turn of one of the burgundy patterns. It still wasn't perfect, but it would have to do. Wiping the greasy sweat from her brow with the back of her palm, she collapsed into the comforting cushions of her sofa, and stared at the rug.

She traced the curling threads of color with her eyes, following them into the weave like secret trails. It reminded her of the time she and Jeremy had hiked in the North Woods, and how he'd lost her when she wasn't looking. He'd stepped off the trail to pee, but after several minutes passed, she followed him into the twisted brush and branches to see what was taking him so long.

When she didn't find him, she'd returned to the trail to wait, but once there, she began to worry that she'd strayed too far from where he'd left her. She'd turned all the way around three and four and five times, peering into the dense brush that closed in the narrow dirt trail. She called out his name, softly at first, and then with increasing urgency.

What if a bear had come up behind him while he was wetting down a treetrunk? It could have happened so fast he wouldn't have had time to cry out, and she wouldn't have heard…

"Boo!" Jeremy yelled, leaping out from behind her.

Jan gasped, grabbed her chest and fell to her knees with the shock.

He apologized, pulling her to her feet and hugging her tightly.

"I thought something had happened," she cried. "A bear or you fell and broke your leg or…"

"No, baby, no… I just wanted to make you jump. I'm sorry. I didn't mean to freak you out that much."

His words and hugs had turned to kisses and caresses. They'd made love in the bushes at the side of the trail. For weeks after, she'd fantasized that the tryst had made her pregnant, until the bleeding began, like clockwork…

Jan pulled her gaze away from the carpet that she was no longer seeing and leaned against the back of the couch, stifling a sob.

The bleeding had always come. And Jeremy had always shaken his head, as if disgusted with her…

Time for bed. When her thoughts turned to this… Jan turned out the light, but didn't rise from the couch. She stared at the wall she couldn't see in the darkness, and cried.

For a week, Jan came home and spent her evenings staring at the rug, memorizing its twists and paths and delicate twinings in her head. While sometimes those intricately threaded trails led her mind to wander down unpleasant paths of its own, mostly, she was happy, lost in the blur of the day's events and the swimming color of dyes. Jan enjoyed the warmth the rug brought to her apartment. Though she couldn't say it had completely filled that empty feeling that came when she stepped in through the door at the end of the day.

The next Thursday, on a whim, she pulled off Glenn Ellyn Road into the parking lot of the carpet shop after work.

She felt lazy, idle. Maybe she'd browse the statuary, or just admire one of the other carpets.

There still was no sign on the door, only the glow of neon tubes to announce that it was a store at all. Jan pulled the door open and stepped inside. The door snapped shut behind her like a trap.

The store was empty.

White walls and beige carpet, fixture on the ceiling without a bulb.

The store had failed fast! she thought, and then considered… it's hard to draw a crowd when you never posted a sign.

"What's on your mind?" a familiar voice said, and the white-haired man seemed to materialize like a light flicked on, from the darkness of the hallway.

"Oh," she said. Jan felt embarrassed for some reason, as if she'd stepped into the man's bedroom and caught him in his stained, torn boxers.

"The store," she said, pausing awkwardly. "didn't do well?"

"Oh, we're doing just fine, ma'am," he answered, and smiled, eyes glinting brightly in the glare of the bulb.

"You just come back when you need something — when you really want something — and we'll have it. I guarantee."

With that, he turned and vanished into the back hallway of the shop.

Jan stood there a moment, almost as lost and disoriented as the last time she'd stepped inside and been overwhelmed by the rugs.

She felt betrayed as she stared at the empty white walls and the boring beige floor.

What kind of game was this guy up to?

She drove home in a kind of shock.

"You just come back when you need something — when you really want something…" she kept hearing in her mind.

When she reached her apartment, she dropped her briefcase on the foyer and kicked her shoes off with force, bouncing one off the wall to land on top of the coffee table. She knelt at the edge of the Oriental rug.

Tears were already starting to run down her face. "I know what I want," she whispered, "I know what I want."

Later that night, after the microwave, after the TV news, after the vodka, Jan climbed back in her car.

"I know what I want," she mumbled, wiping her eyes with the back of her hand.

The store's door slapped shut behind her, and this time she wasn't shocked to see a bare bulb and an empty room.

It wasn't completely empty.

Against the back wall leaned a pickax and shovel, obviously freshly used. There were muddy prints on the banal carpet, dark, dirty footprints that ended in a jumble at the side of the dirt-smeared silver casket. It served as the only furnishing of the otherwise white room.

"You've made up your mind, then," the proprietor said, his voice a cool dagger parting the silence with bloody sound.

Jan was too drunk to cry, too tired to crumble.

"I want Jeremy," she whispered. Then, thinking of the cruel way he'd treated her, blamed her and left her, she corrected herself. "No... I want Jeremy's child."

The nod of his silver hair was almost imperceptible.

"So I surmised."

"Is that... him?" she asked, staring at the casket.

The man nodded. "Is that what you really want?"

"More than anything else."

"Then I will leave you in privacy. You have until midnight." He checked his watch. "Roughly an hour."

"And the cost?" she whispered, already moving forward.

"That you never return," he said, and then vanished once more into the dark hallway.

Jan moved to the edge of the casket. Her eyes wouldn't

stop leaking; the room wouldn't stop shivering beyond the veil of her tears. What if it wasn't him? What if it was him, six months gone?

She pushed at the lid and her hands slipped on the damp earth still smeared on the edge. She pushed again. This time it opened, slowly, with a creak like a door in a haunted house.

It was Jeremy.

His hair, so blond and perfectly coiffed in life, was dulled, dirty, unkempt. His lips, once so full of sarcasm, were pale, lacking in spite or cynicism. His eyes, once electric and sparkling grey, were flat, listless.

But his lips opened when she gasped, and his eyes blinked as she laid her head on his pinstripe-suited chest.

"I love you," she cried, almost incoherent, tears muddying the dust on his deep blue tie.

"And I loved you," he croaked, barely audible in the silence of the empty room.

His arm raised, slowly, hesitantly, like a construction crane that's spent the winter months rusting tight in the yard.

"I wanted to have your child," she cried. "I'm so sorry."

"It was never you," he hissed, and pulled her down into the velvet clutch of the casket with him. *"But I could never admit it."*

* * * * *

Jan never went back to the store with the neon lights. She passed it every day on her way home from work, sometimes noting a car parked there. She wondered what the store held for those patrons, but never dared to stop and find out.

She thought of the store nearly every evening as she sipped warm tea and watched the nightly news and traced the ever-twisting patterns of the deep, dark Oriental carpet with the fingers of her mind.

She smiled a little when she thought of Jeremy. And she cried. But mostly, she just closed her eyes in contentment, and felt the warmth of her belly, and of the child growing so quickly there.

She had what she wanted. And would ask for nothing more.

Christmas, The Hard Way

O ne by one the candles lit, flames flickering into existence without the aid of a match or spark. Will smiled and counted: 25. Perfect. He glanced down the hall to make sure nobody was coming and then smiled a devious grin. Why do it the hard way?

The strand of lights rose like a thin green snake from the bag. Will pointed to the crowning branch of the blue spruce and the strand obeyed. Its end still hidden in the storage bag, as it began to twine around the tree.

On the third loop the plug sailed out of the bag and slapped the wall to mark the wire's last circle about the tree.

Will smiled in appreciation.

No point in getting stuck with pine needles. This was the way to set up Christmas. Flushed with pride, he didn't note the shadow of his father against the wall until his second strand of lights was sailing around the evergreen.

The tree began to turn — without his help. Slowly at first, perfectly matching the spiral of his snaking lights and preventing them from coming to rest on the branches. It spun faster, dislodging bulbs already placed. The tree's motion was matched by a whirlwind that blew Will's long blond hair into his eyes, and his candle flames into oblivion.

Seconds later, the wind and the tree were still, and Will's work undone. Lights lay in tangled heaps on the floor, and the candles hidden throughout the nooks and crannies of the great room were smoking in dark silence.

"Do it right, this time," a familiar voice grated. "Your aunt Ertie will be here soon." His father's heavy steps echoed cruelly through the ruined room as Will stared at the mess.

"Damn, damn, damn!" he hissed, stamping his foot in frustration. Why did they insist on doing things the hard way at Christmas? Wouldn't it be more enjoyable to just get it done? And why did Ertie have to materialize every year? She was so damned annoying. Chatter, chatter, chatter — as if she had a clue what living in today's world was like.

Will shook his head and picked up the nearest plug, shaking the stubborn lights apart one by one to detangle the strand. He'd be here for hours!

At last he found the end of the strand and dragged it to the tree. Stretching on his toes, he tossed it up over the highest branch of the Christmas tree. A needle poked him in the eye. He jerked back, and dropped the lights which fell into a tangle on the ground.

"Damnit!" he snapped aloud.

"It's Christmas, boy, don't swear."

Will turned toward the hallway to see a tiny ghost of a woman, all pale and white-haired. Her glasses perched high on a squat knob of a nose, and hands the color of French vanilla ice cream clung to her barreled hips.

Will bit his tongue and dutifully held his arms out for a chilly hug. He was careful not to clap his arms right through her; she got irritated when he did that.

"Hi Aunt Ertie, when did you get here?"

"When did you start swearing at Christmas?"

"Just now."

"Just so."

He laughed and she flitted away from the perfunctory embrace.

"What are you standing around for? Shouldn't those lights be on the tree instead of the floor? Why aren't the candles lit? You kids today. Lazy and slow."

She winked at him and swooshed back down the hall. Sighing heavily, he turned and started putting up the Christmas decorations… for the third time.

He'd lit the candles — only burning his thumb once — and nearly finished the tree when Janice poked her head into the room.

"Still at it, poky? I finished the dining room half an hour ago!"

Without thinking, Will flicked his hand and across the room an ornament leapt from the decoration box to strike the wall near his younger sister's head.

She laughed and shook her head at the challenge.

"Uh uh. It's Christmas. And I'm telling Dad you used your power."

"Damnit!" he yelled after her. "Who cares?"

Will bent over and plugged the last strand in, then flicked the wall switch to turn the tree on. Hundreds of colored lights blinked on. They shone red and blue and green and gold against the rich hue of the tree. But the subdued beauty of their twinkling was lost on Will.

"Could be brighter," he grumbled.

And grinned. "Sure," he murmured. "Could be brighter!"

He pulled the plug from the wall and touched two fingers to the copper prongs. "Light," he said, and instead got noise.

Pop-pop-pop-pop-pop.

The first strand of Christmas lights exploded from the excessive rush of power he'd unleashed in the wire, showering Will and the room in a mist of colored glass. He felt the bite of tiny barbs on his face and realized his error just as a yell swooped into the room.

"Wiiiilllllll!?"

"Damnit!"

* * * * *

Will slumped on the couch and stared at the squalling infant on his lap. He imagined a honey-coated pacifier and

153

absently popped it into the child's mouth when it appeared. "Why me?" he asked for the hundredth time today. He hated Christmas.

Every year it was the same thing. The family sat down to dinner on the 19th of December and after dessert, his mother would place both palms on the table and say, "It's time. Call your last wishes and then put away your powers. It's Christmas week."

"Couldn't we wait until after the dishes are done?" he'd asked this year, and got a warning swat on the shoulder from Dad.

"That would be missing the point!" his mother replied.

"Well, what is the point?" he'd responded, face twisted in a petulant sneer. "Christmas is a good time for everyone else, but we have to be miserable? Christmas weak — with an A?"

Dad opened his mouth to speak and then, looking much like a gasping goldfish, closed it again.

Mom looked serious. "You think about the point, Will. You think about it while you're doing the dishes. By hand."

* * * * *

The nipple popped out of his baby brother's mouth and Chris began to cry.

"Damnit!" Will snorted. He stood, rocking Chris in his arms. As much as he wished for the kid to shut up, there was no safe way to magic a baby into easing up on the volume. You had to stand up and walk and sing and rock. What a royal pain, he thought, and looked down at the drool-covered chin of his brother. The pink lips bubbled and then opened to let out a piercing cry.

"What do you want?" Will begged. "I can't understand blubbering. Why can't you just tell me? Why do you gotta cry all the time?"

He was still pacing the room with the fidgety baby when

his family returned from their shopping foray into town.

"Gotcha some eggnog," Janice chirped, dashing through the room and into the kitchen. Chris began to wail louder.

"You've got to learn to be gentler with him if you want him to settle," Mom said, dropping a brown bag to the floor and taking the baby from his stiff arms. "You rock him slower, like this."

Will saw how the child folded easily into her arms, how her body swayed softly, so different from his bouncing, impatient movement. Why couldn't he do that?

"And it's no wonder he's crying, Will. He's wet!"

Mom went to change Chris, and Will dropped defeatedly to the couch.

Snow was swirling past the living room window, a shadowy rain in the grey winter evening. Great, he thought dismally. *I'll spend Christmas morning shoveling the driveway.* Why couldn't it wait until after Christmas when he could clear the drive with a wish and a wink?

"Wouldn't be right," rasped a wheezy voice from the couch right beside him. Ertie had the annoying habit of simply being there at all the wrong moments. Will guessed she'd been quite the busybody in life.

"Huh?" he asked, turning to find the piercing gaze of his ghostly aunt upon him.

"Wouldn't be Christmas if you didn't give up somethin'," she said. "You think Christ wanted to leave heaven? You think anybody wants to make a sacrifice? I tell you, when I was a girl, my sister Glennie was always puffing and strutting and getting all the boys. But do you think she got them on her own? Oh no. She tweaked herself with magic. Made 'em think they were licking a gorgeous girl's ear. Meanwhile, I couldn't get a guy for nothing. But did I fake it? Well, once or twice maybe…"

She winked at him, her crow's feet a tide of ripples. "But I knew then what I'm telling you now. Wouldn't be right to get what I wanted that way. Had to sacrifice and get my man on my own call. Because eventually, the glamour won't hide who you are. The magic isn't enough, is what I'm telling you, Will. Ask your aunt Glennie. Ask her why she was never married."

The tiny woman eased herself upright. "I married twice, you know. Twice," she said again, as she faded from the room.

* * * * *

The church was nearly full when they walked into the vestibule at 11:30. Midnight Mass was another Christmas family tradition which Will had grown to hate. The main floor was abuzz with greetings and conversation. A half dozen Christmas trees were scattered about the altar, interspersed with the green and red blossoms of poinsettias in gold-foiled pots.

Pale blue lights wove a fairy dance amid pine boughs on the granite columns lining the main aisle. The muted strains of "Joy To The World" drifted from the organ to add to the chaotic hum.

A balding usher in a lime suit and red Santa tie guided them to the balcony. "Main floor's already packed, folks," he apologized. Will was considering making the garish tie constrict of its own accord when he was swept away by the mob heading upstairs.

The family filed into a pew near the edge of the balcony, first Mom and Chris, then Janice, Ertie, Dad and finally, Will. What a stupid waste of time, he thought, tapping his foot against the kneeler impatiently. As the priest began the mass, Will stared at the lights wound throughout the trees and columns down near the altar. After awhile, he began to reach out with his power to the lights, stopping the current here and there, putting out whole strands and then letting them blink back on. He glanced sideways to see if anyone was watching.

No. Good.

He picked out a handful of lights above the altar and began a wave. He'd shut off one light for a second, then let it back on while knocking out the following color in the strand, and then move on to the next. Anyone watching would see a moving wave of color in the midst of a series of unblinking strands. A miracle, he smiled. He was a miracle worker!

Will was thoroughly enjoying his cleverness when a hand gripped the back of his neck. His dad's voice growled in his ear. "Keep it up, and you won't live to see Christmas," he warned.

Will settled back for the homily.

* * * * *

"What's gotten into you, Will?" Dad asked on the ride home. "Why do you insist on using your power at Christmastime?"

"I just don't see the point," he answered. "Why is Christmas any different than any other time?"

Mom broke in. "It's a symbol, Will. God could have just said 'hey, you're all saved' — but instead, he brought salvation the hard way and became man."

"So how do we know he was God?" Will countered. "Just cuz he could turn water into wine — hell, I can do that!"

The car became deathly silent, and Will realized he'd gone too far. Janice's eyes grew wide as moons from the other side of the backseat. Ertie gazed up at him as if in shock, and then stared into her lap. She looked ashamed of him.

As if he cared what a prune-faced old ghost thought of him.

But if he didn't, why did the look on her face make his chest hurt?

Damnit!

* * * * *

"Merry Christmas," Dad said, raising a glass of egg-nog high in the air. "Merry Christmas!" replied Mom, and Janice, raising their glasses in answer. Will raised his and mouthed the words as well, but they didn't echo warm in his heart as they always had in the past.

Nothing felt right this year. It all seemed a sham. He exaggerated a yawn (which wasn't too hard since it was long after one in the morning) and excused himself for bed. He could feel the eyes of his family following him as he left the kitchen. He knew what they were thinking. *"What's his problem? Why is he trying to ruin Christmas for everyone?"*

"I'm not," he answered the imagined voices. "I'm just trying to find it for myself."

He had just pulled the cool blankets up over his chest when the frizzy white hair of Aunt Ertie materialized next to his bed.

"Can I talk to ya, Will?"

He grunted assent.

Her hair glowed as she moved through the dark room, dipping as she eased herself down on the edge of the bed. He saw the faint shine of her eyes staring down at him and his toes curled. Why couldn't she mind her own business?

"Because I worry about you, that's why!" she answered.

"Stop doing that!" he warned. "I thought the whole point of this Christmas stuff is that we're not supposed to use our powers."

"Hard not to hear you when you're broadcasting gloom and gripe at top volume, boy. Now tell me what it's about. Or snap out of it. You decide. Because I ain't leaving until this is settled. I'm not having you wake up in a black cloud on Christmas morning."

Buzz off you old bag, he thought, before he could stop himself.

"I might remind you that I will use my power again after Christmas is over," she whispered. "Would you like to know what an old bag's powers can do to an insolent, weak, mortal boy?"

Her teeth gleamed as she grinned at the thought.

"No," he said sullenly. "I don't know what's wrong with me. I just can't get into Christmas this year. It all just seems so stupid. I mean, why should I do everything the hard way right at the time when there's so many things to do? Why shouldn't I magic everyone their presents — I could get them stuff they'd want, then. And... I don't know, I just wonder if all this is over some guy who was just like us. Not God at all. Just someone with a little power."

Ertie stroked his cheek with a cool hand. "I'll let you in on a secret, boy. Nobody knows the answer to that last question. But you know what?" She leaned closer. "It doesn't matter."

She grinned again. "Nope, not a bit. Because the magic of Christmas is hidden in your first two questions. And I'll ask you this: what's the point of spell-ing a present for someone who could magic up the same thing without you? There's a reason your mom and dad make you put away your power at Christmas. If it doesn't come from you the hard way, you won't feel nothing at all."

"Well, I got everyone really nice things this year and I bought them myself, I didn't magic them. So why don't I feel good about it?"

"I think you know the answer, boy. Where did the money come from to buy the presents? Did you go to work and sweat for it?"

He didn't answer.

"Will, you make something for your family with your own two hands — you give something of yourself — and you'll have that Christmas feeling you're missing."

"I can't make anything."

"Quit arguing and bellyaching. I'm telling you what you need to do. Either work for it or forget about it. You work for it and I might forget about the 'old bag' crack. Might.

Just remember, Will — there's no easy way out at Christmastime."

She started to fade.

"There's never enough sleep either."

* * * * *

Will lay in bed for a long time after Ertie left the room. Maybe the old apparition had a point. Maybe he had been too lazy this year. But what could he give anybody now? It was too late to build or paint anything — which was how he usually made his holiday offerings. Of course, he did have a new set of pencils he'd been wanting to sketch with. But it was the middle of the night! There were only hours left before they opened presents. What could he draw that he could give to the whole family — because he sure couldn't draw everybody individual things. What did everybody like?

He was already pulling his sketchpad from the closet and searching for his pencils before he decided upon the subject of this sketch. He peeked out into the hallway, making sure everyone had gone to bed. The house was still, dark. He tiptoed down the stairs and worked in the living room for over an hour, lit only by the multicolored glow of the Christmas tree lights. Then he went back upstairs, passed his room and slid softly across the floor of the back bedroom.

He found the barf-cute clown lamp on the dresser and flicked it on, tilting the shade to minimize its brightness. Then he climbed up on the wooden changing table, took a long look at his drooling, rosy-cheeked baby brother and began to draw, pencils shading black and grey in the quiet, dim light of Christmas morning.

* * * * *

Will was bleary-eyed as the family gathered around the tree in the morning.

But he was smiling. Sometime during the night his frustration and ennui over the holiday had lifted.

"Who's going first?" Dad asked as he sank into the couch.

"I will," Janice called and crawled under the bottom boughs of the tree, catching her candycane nightgown in the branches to expose her flowered underwear. "Ahhh!" she cried and backed out, shaking the tree and knocking off an ornament in her hurry.

"Here, Will." She handed him a small box and pulled her nightgown back down around her legs. He yanked at a loose edge and tore the paper from the box. It said Carson Pirie Scott, but he knew it couldn't be something from the mall. Anyway, it was too heavy for clothes. Will slid a fingernail across the edge of the lid to slit the tape, and flipped off the cover. The scent of fresh cut wood rose immediately from the open box, and he pulled out a smooth deep-grained wooden frame.

"Dad helped me make it," Janice smiled at his own grin. "Remember when we were at the store yesterday? We stopped at Mr. Isner's and used his special saw to make the edges. But I found the wood from a dead tree in the forest. I cut it and stripped off the bark and everything."

"Thanks, Janice," Will said, his chest warming suddenly. "I think I have just the thing to put in it."

He reached behind the tree and pulled out another box. "Mom, Dad, this is for everyone. I had other presents under here for you guys, but it was just store stuff. I made this for the family last night."

Mom and Dad looked at him quizzically a moment, and then pulled the paper off together, with Janice huddled up against their legs by the couch to see. Dad pulled the lid from the box and they all stared inside.

"Oh, Will," Mom said, lifting the picture out. "It's wonderful!"

"This is the best thing you've drawn," dad declared.

"Why are my eyes closed?" Janice asked, unimpressed.

"Because you were sleeping at four o'clock this morning," he answered.

"Look, Ertie," Mom said, holding the picture for the matriarchal ghost. Ertie stared at the picture a moment and grinned.

"You figured if you put an old bag at the top she wouldn't turn you into a tree come tomorrow, eh, boy?"

Will laughed and handed over his new frame. "Put it in here. I think it will fit."

Janice helped, and in a minute, held up the result for all to admire. The family Christmas tree filled the majority of the frame, but beneath its branches lay baby Chris, wrapped in a blanket, hands clenched in tiny fists. Scattered throughout the tree were four ornaments, but they weren't just globes. Etched upon their round surfaces were the tranquil, sleeping faces of Mom, Dad, Janice and Will. The angel atop the tree's crown bore an unmistakable resemblance to a certain hazy aunt.

"Understand now?" Ertie asked quietly, so only he could hear.

"Yeah. Thanks."

Janice pulled down an old picture from the living room wall to hang the new one. Will stifled a yawn with his fist, and stared at the tree. A rainbow of colors glittered softly against the blue-green boughs, while snow flew past the window outside.

After some consideration, Will decided the Christmas tree lights were bright enough after all.

The Humane Way

It's a shame it had to be this way," Barbara said, slipping a thin sliver of white meat from the platter to her mouth. Al was a sucker for stuffing, but she had to admit, she loved the meat.

"It's dry and tasteless without gravy," he often complained, which she once took as a slur on her competence as head cook of the Ardmore household. Later she'd realize it was an avoidance based on more than tastebuds. At heart, Al was really a tunnel-visioned moralist.

"But what were we to do?" she continued, setting the last dish for Christmas dinner on the table. "This is the best meat we can afford."

Mrs. Holzman from next door had joined them, now that her Fred was six months under-the-sod and her kids emigrated to Quebec. They didn't enforce the one-child procreation laws there. Typical of the egocentric French. To hell with the rest of the world, we want to breed. Barbara's own daughter, Amy, was still at Gibson Virtual Tech, but that would be remedied in a moment.

The long, loaded platter fit perfectly on the table next to the ornate blue china gravy bowl. She was most proud of her setting this evening. The tablecloth was a finely woven pattern of silver threaded ivy. The china plates had waves of blue-stalked wheat on their edges. And the silverware gleamed invitingly, thanks to the warm yellow glow of the candelabra. They didn't make utensils like that anymore; delicate filigrees of blooming flowers exploded up the shafts of each piece.

It was all hand-me-down treasures from Grandma. Barbara's four siblings had gotten the house and cars and insurance money, but she was happy to keep her grandma's kitchen things. They reminded her of the crowded family feasts when her parents were alive. They made dinner an extra sensual experience and Barbara saved them for special.

"Have you called Amy, yet?" Al asked, already pulling the heaping mountains of mashed potatoes towards him. The man couldn't wait when food was at issue.

She shook her head and walked over to the stairs, punched the well-fingered white button there. "Dinner," she called.

"Mom," whined a disembodied shrill voice from the tiny speaker. "Why must you always bother me like this! I'm at college!" Her voice dropped to a whisper, "and I'm with *Doug.*"

"Amy, it's Christmas. You have no classes today. Quit fooling around and come to dinner!"

"But mom…"

"No buts! This is a family day. Now let's go. I want your feet. The real ones, not the virtuals. Under the table. Now."

She punched the button a second time, breaking the connection, and returned to the table. She stood there a moment, taking it all in. Wondering what she might have missed. With Mrs. Holzman there, she wanted this Christmas dinner to be extra special. A feast of celebration to take the old woman's mind off her missing kids and husband.

A whoosh of air from behind her, a blur of purple lips and plastic yellow headgear and Amy plopped into the seat across from her father. "Merry Christmas everyone," she chirped, cocking her head up to smirk at her mother. "Did I miss the presents? I feel like I've been away at college for sooo long."

"Spare the sarcasm, Amy," Al growled. "You know a virtual diploma is just as good as one from an ivy-grower. Those places are too crowded and we can't afford to send you away. You haven't exactly slaved away to pay for it yourself. Now lose the connection."

Frowning, Amy flipped up the lenses and pulled off the headpiece to reveal a crop of flouncing black hair and soft brown eyes. It wasn't exactly how she portrayed herself in virt to Doug at Gibson, but she'd probably never meet him fleshwise, anyway. Hell, his piercing baby blues and shock blond hair probably had the help of some virt touchup of his own, she was sure.

"You know, I *could* get a job as a netbabe and make lots of money for real college," she threatened.

Al's baldspot colored at the thought of his daughter offering virtsex to strangers because he couldn't afford to send her to an ivy-grower college. "No daughter of mine..."

Barbara broke in and shooshed them both. "Enough you two. It's Christmas and time to give thanks for all we do have. Now join hands and let's say grace. Al?"

He picked up her lead and began, his heavy voice weighting each word with import. That was one of the reasons Barbara had first dated him — when he spoke, well, it could just give you chills. How could kids today duplicate that on headgear? When anyone could be, well, *anyone*?

Al took Barbara's hand on his left and Mrs. Holzman's on his right. Amy slapped Mrs. Holzman five before clasping her thin, well-veined claws. The old woman couldn't help but grin.

"Father, thank you today for this feast in your memory," Al's basso-rich voice began. "May we treasure each bite as if it were manna from your heaven. May we always be blessed as we are today with a warm hearth, a healthy body and our family all around us. May the love we seek be true and our ends ease our spirits gently back to you. And thank you Lord, in your wisdom, for sparing us our children."

Barbara gave him a look sharper than the carving knife she held to divvy up the roast. Al had already filled his plate with potatoes, stuffing and beans.

"How is school going, dear?" asked Mrs. Holzman, ladeling milky brown gravy over her potatoes. Barbara cooked them with the skins on, letting them swim and soften in butter and chives before mashing them. Amy loved them that way. So much so that the current dollop of potatoes threatened to eclipse the rest of her plate.

"Save room for the rest of your dinner," her mom laughed, and answered the older woman herself. "We're so proud of her! Amy got a 3.6 average last semester. She aced Virtual Morality and even got an A in her Offline Sociology class."

Mrs. Holzman nodded encouragingly.

Al muttered, "What do you expect when she was raised with a computer in the crib?"

"Dad still thinks that people should actually be in the same room with each other to have a conversation," Amy laughed. "Can you imagine?"

"Well, that is the way things used to be," the older woman sighed. She absently pushed the heavy plastic glasses up her nose and then dropped her gaze to the tablecloth, instantly undoing the adjustment. "There's something to be said for real human contact. Can't make babies without it."

"Well, isn't that *exactly* the problem?" Amy countered, warming to the discourse. "I mean, if your generation hadn't *made* so many babies, we wouldn't be in the mess we're in now."

Barbara pursed her lips and passed the platter to Al.

"That was only part of the problem, honey," Barbara said. "Remember the rampant salmonella outbreaks of the teens. And then the double helix livestock virus after that. It's not so much that there were too many of us, it's more that the viruses got smarter and our food supply started drying up. Dying down, really."

"We could've just become vegetarians," Al grunted, passing the plate to Mrs. Holzman.

Barbara laughed derisively and reached out to pat her husband's ample middle.

"Yeah, I can see you giving up meat for good."

Mrs. Holzman cleared her throat faintly as she picked a thin bit of white meat and passed the platter on to Amy. The wrinkled jowls under her chin wobbled as she spoke. "If the laws had been the same when I was younger, I wouldn't have been allowed to keep my Jenny. Not that it matters now. She and Rog won't ever come back to this country. They've each gone and had three kids."

Her pale blue eyes fogged up and she avoided the stare of her hostess. "The one-child laws didn't keep me from having my kids then, but they've sure taken 'em both away now."

Barbara dropped her silverware to the plate with a clink that made everyone at the table look up. That was the last straw. She had gone down to the supermarket, picked out a good plump 10 pounder (a pinch on the thigh and she knew this one would be tender) and slaved all day in the kitchen to make this a special dinner. She would not have her family pull the gloom down over their heads and spoil the meal.

She stood up, put a hand on her hip and raised a stern finger at all of them. "Now look. We can't live on potatoes, rice and beans all our lives, and people are threatening to outnumber the ants on this earth. The one-child laws are fair and necessary."

"And dreamed up by some freak in a computer somewhere," Al mumbled. "Nobody could have come up with it if they'd been in the same room eye-to-eye with a mother."

Barbara ignored him and turned her attention to the older woman, who sunk deeper into her chair. "I'm sorry Mrs. Holzman, but nobody needs more than one child and it's a shame Jenny and Rog can't see that. It's dangerous for all of us on this earth, whether they live here — or in Quebec — to have more than one child. We have to cut our population and conserve our resources or we will all starve. This is the best way. It's the most *humane*."

Mrs. Holzman looked chastised. Al stared down at the half-cut strips of meat on his plate. Amy rolled her eyes.

"Now we are blessed today, on Christmas, with this bountiful feast. I'll remind you that Mary only had one child. The least we can do is enjoy this dinner in her honor. Somebody put in nine months to bring it to us. We will *not* let it go to waste."

She looked at Amy's meatless plate overflowing with potatoes and gravy and thrust the steaming platter of tender baby roast, still redolent with the marinade of oregano, sherry and garlic, back at her daughter.

"Arm or leg?"

The Right Instrument

J ack's elbows slammed on the plastic synthesizer keys in defeat, earning a chaotic crash from the speakers.

Every C major chord diminished to an A minor, every G to an E flat minor. His stalled jingle for Carter's Beans was a lamed "Sunrise, Sunset."

"It's Karen's fault," he'd bitched at Crazy Eddie. "I can't write without her. I need her to make music now."

Three months ago, Karen had pushed Jack over for an aerobics instructor. Since then, his freelance jingle-writing business had hit the skids big time. Who wanted to try selling products with tunes that made consumers wanna cry?

Eddie had only nodded in that crazy way he had, shag carpet eyebrows waffling creepily.

"All you need is the right instrument," he'd said.

* * * * *

Jack stared at the Korg M-1 beneath his elbows and shook his head. There was nothing wrong with the instrument. The problem was him. His head. His inability to get over the fact that the best thing that had ever happened to him was over. Done. Screwing another guy.

After their breakup, Jack had begged for another chance. Her eyes answered with the sort of look you'd give a mortally wounded dog. "I can't, Jack," was all she'd say.

She wouldn't even return calls anymore. Lately, messages on her answering machine brought no reply, but as he hung up the phone each time, he could hear her saying it, over and over.

"I can't, Jack."

The doorbell rang, and with a groan, Jack shoved himself up.

Crazy Eddie's too-close eyes and skewed nose peered distortedly through the door's peephole.

"Why am I friends with this nutcase?" Jack asked himself for the thousandth time, but turned the knob. If nothing else, Eddie was loyal.

Strange. Twisted. But loyal as a hound.

"Got something for you, Jack." Eddie motioned to someone outside. "Bring it!"

"What's going on?"

"You needed the right instrument, so I made it for you."

Four grunting men carried it through Jack's door.

"Next to the other one," Eddie pointed toward the keyboard. They set down an upright piano, brought in a bench and left.

"Sit," Eddie commanded. "Play."

It was a beautiful instrument, stained a deep oak and glossed with rich varnish. The keys themselves, though slightly notched and uneven at their edges, had not yet yellowed with age. They were obviously newer than the rest of the piano. A reconditioned antique?

"Eddie, this is too much, really! It must have cost…"

"Play, Jack. It was cheap. I bought it from a junkshop, refinished it and carved new keys myself."

Still unsure, Jack touched the keys. A deep F chord emerged. Then a bright G. The tones were marvelous! Jack smiled and launched a complex run of scalar ascensions.

He lost himself in the warmth of the sound and unconsciously slid into the stalled bean jingle. Instead of slumming in minor keys, however, he suddenly knew the transition it needed and instantly, the tune clicked.

"This is amazing, Eddie! I've been dicking around with this jingle for a week, and there it is, just like that.!"

"You just needed the right instrument." Eddie winked.

* * * * *

One week passed, and then another. Jack's love for the piano crescendoed. Maybe he'd just become incapable of working on sterile synthesizers, he mused. The feel of running his fingers over the heavy keys, their resistance and tactile differences — they changed the experience of playing for him.

The now-jaunty bean jingle sold, which allowed him to just make his rent payment.

More and more catchy hooks rolled off his fingers to the keys every day. He could barely get one written down before another idea struck.

When Crazy Eddie stopped by again, Jack greeted him with a bear hug. "Thanks Eddie, really. I guess I didn't need Karen around at all. I just needed a new instrument."

Eddie's lips split apart for a crooked smile. "No," he said. "You needed the *right* instrument. A keyboard that kept Karen close to you at all times."

Jack frowned. "What are you talking about?"

"I told you I carved all those keys myself, Jack. But I didn't tell you out of what. And I certainly can't afford ivory."

Jack turned to the piano, eyes squinting in confusion at the rippled, uneven row of creamy keys.

"Then… what?"

"I strangled her with piano wire. It was easy. It seemed appropriate. She was meant for this, for you. I carved her bones smooth as balsa.

"Now every note you play channels through Karen."

Jack gasped, and Eddie patted him on the back.

"She sounds good, doesn't she?"

Vigilantes of Love

Detective Ribaud hated the mornings after.
After the full moon.
Once the inspiration of lovers, the full moon now filled hearts with fear. The curse of the moon had crept through the low buzz of the swampy bayou for decades. Its expanding, deadly army inspired – enforced – faithfulness with their unflinching retribution.

"Was it...?" the woman asked. Her eyes were red-rimmed and swollen; her arms crossed protectively over the heavy swell of her chest. She still wore a thin nightgown, stuck to her wide thighs with the early sweat of a Louisana dawn. Curls of her salt and pepper hair crushed unevenly around her broad face. Madelaine Mendel was not a beautiful woman, which would not help her in her new status. That of the recently widowed.

Ribaud stroked a black goatee and peered in at Mrs. Mendel's bed. The bedspread and top sheet were piled at its foot, exposing a long dark smear of crimson that glistened wetly on one side of the white bottom sheet. The other side of the bed was unmarked.

"Was it...?" the woman asked him for the second time.

"I'm afraid so," he nodded grimly. "You say you heard and felt nothing?"

"No," she squawked, shaking her head in emphasis. Mrs. Mendel put a tissue to her nose and blew loudly before continuing. Her voice was shrill. "We went to bed around eleven, like usual, and when I woke up..."

She broke into a fresh flurry of sobs.

Ribaud patted her shoulder with a calloused palm. "It's hard, I know," he said. This was the fourth house he'd visited since starting his shift, and the morning was young. He had yet to find a corpse; there'd be none and no one to arrest for murder. But he'd seen plenty of blood. That was the way they worked. They didn't just take vengeance, they took bodies.

"But, if it was them…" she snuffled, casting a bleary but desperate eye at the detective. "…that means my Harry was…"

"That's just a superstition, ma'am," he said. "We don't know why they take who they do." His voice sounded hollow. According to the superstition that he and most of New Orleans firmly believed, there was only one reason why the army of the moon came and killed.

Legend said they killed to protect the sanctity of love.

Legend said they came from a misused charm of the voodoo priestess Marie Laveau in the 1800s.

Legend said they only took those who'd defiled that most sacred of bonds.

Supposedly, the curse originated with a spurned wife who sought revenge on her betrothed for his lustful indiscretions. She begged Laveau for an untraceable way to punish him for his betrayal. She also insisted that his heart be crushed, and that his lifeless body be made to wander the bayou forever, punishing others who had stooped to similar crimes against the heart.

For years the people of the swamps had whispered of the killers that walked by the light of the full moon, only taking the hearts and bodies of the impure of heart. Now the army had moved into the city to take those who sullied the vows of love where they lay in their beds, sleeping the sleep of the adulterous under the baleful eye of the full moon. No corpses or body parts were ever left behind, only the stain of blood from where their hearts were ripped out. And those who were taken joined the legions who lurched out of and back into the swamps on the night of the full moon each month.

Every month their numbers grew.

Every month the cries from those who woke on blood-ied beds grew louder.

The curse had become a plague.

Next month, the rotting corpse of Harry Mendel would shamble at midnight through the Quarter, or the Garden District, looking for someone with a black stain marring the heart. And he would kill and keep that heart when he found it.

"It was probably a one-time thing," he said to the sob-bing woman, still trying to comfort her. She would never know for sure, and it would eat at her heart forever.

Ribaud knew.

He'd woken up alone to a red smear on his bedsheets a year ago. He'd known that his beautiful Emily was a tease and a flirt, but he'd always believed it went no farther than that.

The blood on his bed said otherwise.

Ribaud stepped out of Mrs. Mendel's tiny frame house and took a breath of thick air. The sound of sirens called from all around. If one stood and listened, the cries of lovers lost echoed the alarms.

It was time to pay a visit to Eleanor. This couldn't go on much longer, or there'd be no one left.

Eleanor Trevail ran Eleanor's Arcana, a Voodoo shop just off Bourbon Street. It was a favorite destination for tourists who found its bags of white and orange powders (*Love Potion #6, Intellect Enhancing Tea, Spirit Deflector Talc*) amusing and kitschy. They also found Eleanor's storefront sign, promising advice on shamanism, alchemy and spiri-tuality, among other disciplines, a great backdrop for their cameras.

But New Orleans natives knew that Eleanor's store of-fered much more than a photo opportunity and a bag of oddly labeled tea to take home to the family as a souvenir. Eleanor was the real deal in modern Voodoo queens. She had studied all of the arcane notes and journals and spells of Laveau. She had travelled among the practitioners in the Louisiana bayou, dancing naked with snakes and fire at midnight. Once, without warning, she had disappeared and stayed gone for weeks without explanation. When she returned, people said her black skin seemed to gleam with an even deeper ebon energy than before. Of that trip she would only say that she had been to Africa.

Ribaud moved quickly down Bourbon towards the Arcana. He had worked the Bourbon beat half his life, helping cordon off the street and herd the alcohol-hazed revelers close to the streetside bars, away from the dark and dangerous sidestreets. Evil lurked in the Quarter at night, and not just the spiritual variety. Where there were tourists, there were thieves, and the best way to avoid filing paperwork on a parade of slit-throat bodies was to stop those bodies from ever venturing near where their throats might get slit.

Angel, Eleanor's most promising acolyte, smiled at him as he shoved aside the beads that bordered the store's entrance, and stepped inside. A low haze of flutes and airy piano filled the store.

The young clerk moved to meet him. "Haven't seen you out this way in a few," she said, brushing a wild strand of red hair from her eye.

"Been too busy cleaning up the stiffs." He raised an eyebrow and nodded at the back room where the bags of magical talismans and potions were ground up and packaged.

"She around?"

Angel shrugged. "Haven't seen her today. She left early last night to meet someone for dinner at Arnaud's. She's probably at home with a sore head."

Ribaud laughed, trying to imagine the cool stare of the stoic Voodoo priestess with a drunken hangover.

"Yeah, right," he said. "Well, if you see her…"

"I'll tell her you were sniffing around."

"Do."

Ribaud fingered a love charm hanging on a rack filled with little sachets. Rose petals and exotic herb leaves rustled in the white silken bag. A sign at the top of the display said, "Make Sure Your Lover Stays True. Love Potion #8."

"Surprised you still have any of these left," he said.

She crinkled her nose.

"People figure they don't need them now. If your girlfriend or boyfriend cheats on you, someone will come along and rip out their heart. What better guarantee of fidelity is there than that?"

"The logic makes sense," he agreed, "but it doesn't seem to be working." He waved behind him as he left the store.

Bourbon was quiet as Ribaud sauntered down its rough cobblestones, the smell of last night's stale beer still thick in the air. On his left, an old man hosed down the tile in front of a narrow streetside bar. A scum of foam washed into the gutter and down a sewer hole.

Ribaud looked up and saw the sign for the Lust Is Life Condom Company, just a few calculated steps from the Temptations strip club. He was surprised either one of them had managed to keep their doors open over the past few months. But while Bourbon's lascivious devil-may-care party attitude had dampened, so far the curse hadn't put it out. Every night the jazz and blues spilled out of the clubs and into the street along with a host of tourists and locals, all looking for a good time. Not even the threat of death could slow the search for the pleasures of the flesh.

He walked back to his squad and decided to take a ride over to Eleanor's house. Bourbon wasn't dead yet, but at the rate things were going, it wouldn't be long. And her Voodoo might be the city's only hope.

The road to Eleanor's wound beneath a canopy of cypress branches and grey moss, through a maze of sloughs and swamps and overgrown ponds. While her business was, necessarily, in the city, her real work was done here. To commune with the spirits of nature, one had to actually spend some time there.

Ribaud had first met Eleanor after Emily was taken. He'd been depressed and nearly suicidal at the time, and took a leave of absence from the force. He'd spent hours hanging over the second story balconies on Bourbon, drinking himself into oblivion. He watched the rowdy women from New York and Los Angeles and Chicago holding up their tank tops to earn strands of beads in response to calls of "show us your tits." Most would wake with headaches the next day and little idea of what they'd done the night before. And most would be gone long before the night of the full moon. They escaped the retribution his Emily had not.

One afternoon while wandering the still-quiet street, he'd poked a bleary head into Eleanor's Arcana and idly ran his hands across the bags of powders and talismans of bone and feather.

"Do you have one to bring back the dead?" he'd asked, a challenge in his voice, but desperation in his eye.

A woman with skin the color of deepest chocolate flashed a smile that held no humor. "We do not speak of such things," she said.

"My wife was killed by a curse," he said, "and I want her back. Isn't that the point of Voodoo?"

"Tell me more about your wife," the woman said.

He had.

He'd told her about the way Emily had looked up at him through lashes black as pitch. He'd told her about the way she had pursed her lips in a moue that could make men laugh, melt and cry all at once. He'd told her about the night they pledged their love in the reeds at Standing Point, their voices barely audible above the hum of the locusts and cries of the nightbirds.

"If she loved you so much, she would still be yours," Eleanor suggested.

"Everybody can make a mistake," he answered. "She was a creature of the senses, always at war with her desires.

But in her heart, she always was mine."

Eleanor said nothing.

"If you are a Voodoo queen, why don't you stop this curse?" he'd asked. "It's killing more and more innocent people every month."

"They're not innocent," she whispered.

"They don't deserve to die," he said.

He'd left Eleanor's shop angry that day, but he'd soon returned. An idea had hatched in his mind, and he couldn't let it go. He began to drink less, and lobby Eleanor more. He got up in the mornings looking forward to the day's debate at her shop. They'd talk for hours about Voodoo, morality, the curse, and its punishments.

Eventually, she agreed to seek a way to stop the curse, though grudgingly, as it was not a spell of her own spinning. She said she might be able to find a way to halt its spread, but warned that she could never bring back his Emily.

Last week, she'd thought she was close. He'd stopped by the Arcana after work and she had run out to him from the back room, holding a yellowed scroll in one hand and what looked like a rotted turnip in the other.

"This could be the key!" This time, her smile was not cool. "I've been looking into some of the things I brought back from Africa, and I think that if I can get one last ingredient, I might be onto something."

Ribaud pulled his squad down the rutted path that led to Eleanor's house. It hid beneath the emerald shadows of a forest of heavy branches. Eleanor lived where life was always ripe. Nature overran every attempt by man to tame it here, and that was exactly where she had wanted to live. At a nadir of natural energy.

He knocked on the old wood door, and at his touch, it fell open, letting a thin slice of sun slip inside.

"Eleanor?" he called.

There was no answer.

He stepped inside. The hum of the swamp faded away.

"Eleanor?" he called again, and stepped into the living room. Voodoo masks and shelves filled with all nature of colored vials adorned the walls. The room was painted a deep red, and above a small brick fireplace was an array of statuary, naked brown voodoo women carved in mahogany, and demon serpents wrought in stone. An obsidian knife lay on the wooden floor, blade pointing into the dark hole of the fireplace.

The kitchen counters were empty of food or spell, and Ribaud stepped through the dining room and into the dark shadows of the hall. Even in the full light of day, the sun never found a hold inside Eleanor's house.

Hers was a citadel of night. A church of the moon.

Grit cracked under his shoes as he stepped into the arch of her bedroom. A yellowed shade covered most of the one window in the room, but there was enough light to see the dark stain across the unmade bed.

"She's gone," a tired voice said from his left. It came from a shadowed form sitting in a small wooden chair just beyond the window.

"Who're you?" Ribaud asked, startled.

"It doesn't matter," the low voice sighed. "I loved her. And now they've taken her."

Ribaud looked from the shadow in the chair to the stain on the bed. In all his visits with her, Eleanor had never mentioned a man in her life. Let alone men.

"She came home late last night," the man said. "And this morning she was gone. Was she with you?"

The chair creaked as the man slowly levered himself upright. He was a big man, a man of iron power, but Ribaud wasn't afraid. He could see the light in those dark eyes was gone.

"No," Ribaud said. "Not with me. I came to see if she had gotten closer to curing this curse." He paused, but the man didn't react. "It took my wife, too," he added.

The man laughed then, a low, tortured gasp.

"There is no cure for love," the man said, and sank back in his chair. He turned his head to stare out the thin slit of glass not covered by the shade.

"And there is no cure for lust, either."

Ribaud stepped back out of the room and into the hall. The house still sheltered the fetid smell of them. The hall and bedroom were ripe with the stink of rotting detritus, the scum that slimed the banks of a swamp.

It stank of the shallow water stirred by the bubbles of decay at high noon in summer. The smell was anchored in the footsteps leading to and away from the bed. Already drying to a mottled grey, the swamp mud from the feet of Eleanor's killer led through the living room and out the front door. A black-green smear coated the doorknob and the wood surrounding it.

A tear bled to his chin as Ribaud retraced his steps and left the house of Eleanor Trevail, the most powerful Voodoo priestess in all of New Orleans.

There would be no stopping Marie Laveau's misbegotten curse.

There would be no stopping the growing army of the moon.

There would be no stopping the fickle human heart.

They had come and gone again, and there would be no cure.

Ribaud would continue to clean up the blood in their wake, until there were no hearts left to break. In twenty-nine more days, they would be back.

The Vigilantes of Love.

LOST STORIES:

Rescued Vigilantes

T here were a number of stories that ended up on the cutting room floor when we were putting the original *Vigilantes of Love* trade paperback together. Not because they weren't decent tales, but because the goal of that original series of Twilight Tales single author collections was to produce *thin* trade paperbacks. Back in the days of actual paper books, print got expensive. And *Vigilantes*, even with its original contents of 15 stories, was already larger than intended.

As I put together this 10th Anniversary edition, I thought it would be nice to include a handful of those "lost" stories, which have never been collected in my subsequent short story collections.

"Learning To Build" was accepted in May 1993, right after "Preserve," but actually ended up claiming the title as my first "published" story in a genre magazine (it beat "Preserve" to the streets by a few weeks).

"Tunnel" was a very early story that was written as a lark. Science fiction magazines in the early '90s frequently had these humorous flash fiction "science" joke style stories, and this was my attempt to write one. I wrote it in 1993, while I was compiling a bunch of my high school and college stories and poems together in a little chapbook that I printed up just for me and a couple friends — sort of a personal time capsule. I titled that chapbook *Tunnels* and actually several of the stories in it saw print in indie magazines before the title story did. Similarly, the story "Key To Her Heart" was sold to a magazine called *Haunts* in the '90s... but then after waiting for a couple years for it to appear, the magazine went on hiatus... and then never returned; the story did finally did see print in another magazine, but not until the 2000s.

"Tomatoes" is just a fun summer horror tale, and "Hair of the Dog" was actually the first in a series of fantasy stories I wrote for *Sirius Visions* magazine in the '90s about kids who get embroiled in the drama of a race of goblins who live beneath their feet. I've since put that series of stories together in a middle grade novel, which I hope will see print one of these days — preferably before my son is too old to read them!

Finally, "Why Do You Stay With Him?" is a humorous flash fiction flipside to my story "Anniversary," which appeared in *Cage of Bones*.

I always regretted that "Hair of the Dog" and "Key To Her Heart," in particular, didn't end up in *Vigilantes*, so I hope you'll enjoy those and the rest of these anniversary edition "extras."

Hair of the Dog

"Climb the rope now, you little coward!"

Billy Knocker looked on helplessly as Coach Gillis bullied Tommy into shimmying up the heavy braided cord. Up a rope which reached all the way to the dark, shadowy rafters of the gym ceiling. Up a rope which Coach Gillis knew Tommy was terrified of.

Billy clenched his fists in anger for his friend. Gillis was constantly torturing his son like this in front of the class. Taunting him, yelling at him, making him go first in any activity which could conceivably bring Tommy's timidness out on display for all to see.

Gripping the rope after Coach's latest stream of abuse, Tommy's face reflected a tangled mix of terror, helplessness and resignation as his wiry biceps bulged and his feet left the ground.

Billy vowed at that moment that somehow, he'd get Coach Gillis for doing this to Tommy. A few feet away, the balding gym teacher grinned a shark's spread of teeth and announced to the rest of the class: "see, it's easy. Even a *baby* can do it!"

* * * * *

Arrshgran visualized the mayhem he'd planned with unconcealed glee. A twist of the wind and the thermos rolled so. Augmented with the spell of weight, it jarred the wheelbarrow, knocking it over. The load of wet concrete shifting so quickly unbalanced the scaffold, (weakened secretly this morning with file and stone). Another twist of the wind — and *crash*. The whole works would slam into the freshly laid brick wall, sending the humans careening through air and the dislodged bricks tumbling to earth atop them. A worthy, if not entirely original, offering for Grretherin.

The goblin peered out from the shade of a decaying public mailbox across the street from the building. His ears kept brushing the underside of the fading blue and red box, knocking loose repeated rains of rust. He shook them from his head in irritation. Time for the wind.

Arrshgran closed his eyes, concentrated, reached out with a finger of mind. His vision expanded, allowing him to see the harmonic crosspoints of air. With a psychic punch, he harangued the current into spasm. Just enough to get the thermos rolling. But as the thermos launched into motion, he realized he'd done it backwards. He'd forgotten to cast the spell of weight.

The silver bullet was picking up speed, moving across the platform, the bricklayers oblivious to the danger of its intent behind them. Arrshgran twisted a finger, tapped a foot, spit on a rock. In a fury of haste, he lofted the spell with a thrust of his palms at the pinnacle object in his plan. He was too late. As the thermos made contact with the barrow, it bounced off harmlessly, gaining the mass of an elephant a moment *later* and plummeting over the side of the scaffold. The wildly overweight thermos breached the concrete sidewalk, embedding in the earth a foot below with a crunch of broken glass.

Arrshgran scratched his wart-ridden nose. Snorted. Dug a trench through the waxy buildup in his ear canal. What else could he use as the trigger? His foot tapped angrily on the cracked grey earth with an anxious *thud, thud, thud*. And then his fist pounded the bottom of the mailbox, which rewarded him in a hollow tang and a rain of brown flakes. His swarthy dark skin was now fashionably dusted in orange. He sneezed.

The bricklayers had descended to the ground now, his opportunity, for the moment, stalled. They stared into the hole, and then looked in unison five stories up to their perch. "What were you drinking for lunch?" one asked the other. Before the thermos owner could answer, a screech of brakes sent the men diving back from the edge of the street. A dent-weathered taxi had cut off a large green Buick, which leapt onto the sidewalk and stopped with a tap against the scaffold. The bumper of the Buick wasn't scratched, but the kiss was all it took. With a gently crescendoing groan, the temporary structure began to lean. Faster and louder it creaked, tools and other debris clinking and clonking to the street in a metallic shower. The scaffold itself crashed harmlessly on the sidewalk. The driver apologized, the bricklayers congratulated each other on their fortune, and the goblin prince Arrshgran, unnoticed by all, screamed a wail of hatred.

* * * * *

Billy Knocker launched the lit pack of firecrackers through the open window and dashed for cover. He was still running for the evergreen he'd picked as a base when it went off *bang bang bang, pop, bang bang,* but was breathlessly in place when the bald pate of Coach Gillis appeared in the window, yelling and shaking his fist at an empty yard. Perfect toss! He counted to 100 after Gillis, grumbling and shaking his beefy round face, turned away and disappeared into the shadowed depths of the house once more. Then he lit another wick, tossed it at the window, and this time, kept on running past his evergreen base. It would probably only take two tosses, he figured. Then the fat old jerk would be huffing and hollering his way up and down the block.

He circled the MacKenzie's house, hopped a fence, and peered from their back yard across the street to Gillis'. No bellering. No stomping up and down the asphalt. Gillis had simply slammed shut the window.

Nips! He'd wanted to get the guy going. Billy stole back

out of the yard and headed towards the park. It was getting late and he'd have to get home soon, but dusk always seemed the best time for catching crayfish.

* * * * *

Arrshgran watched the human boy hunched over the stream with renewed hope. Yellow shorts, a dirty white shirt portraying giant turtles with bandannas, blonde hair, freckles, blues eyes. The kid was perfect. Eight, ten, twelve — Arrshgran could never judge human age well, but he'd place this kid on the upper end of that range. But what to use? So far today, he'd attempted the elaborate construction site fete, only to have it fizzle. Then he'd attempted a life spell on the food in a restaurant, only to have it deflected somehow to a sparrow which had evidently broken its neck on the restaurant's front window. The rising flurry of a formerly ex- bird was hardly the effect he'd been looking for. But now, another chance. The boy. Arrshgran preferred rattling elders — you could generally get much more dramatic effect from the older folk — but he was running out of time. Perhaps a transformation spell. What could he give a small boy that would be obvious, horrifying, and yet, not so debilitating that said youth wouldn't be able to make it back home? Where, if Arrshgran planned this aright, the boy would be the subject of jibes and ridicule for years to come. The idea suddenly came to him. Ah, that would be a delicious *religctaud*. He spoke the spell:

> *"Growing as fast as the river beside*
> *Seeking the ground like a rabbit its lair*
> *from every pore where the sweat may reside*
> *grow me Herculean hair!"*

He stared at the boy now, watching for the change. Arrshgran's scaly black tongue darted from tooth to tooth seeking a lost morsel to enjoy as he savored this outer moment. Which, he realized with a new wrinkle in his already well-furrowed head, did not seem to be too quick in coming. He considered the spell and its diction. Using human references was most powerful in a spell for humans, which was why he had inserted the Hercules thing. And he had mentally thrown it right at the boy.

Who was now rising in the air. Billy's own blond ruffle was not growing visibly at all, but the moss on the tree behind him was — its hairy green fingers rushed from tree-trunk to ground and had slid right underneath the boy's haunches. When the quickly growing moss began ascending once more, Billy was, like it or not, along for the ride.

The goblin swore, a vile, wicked curse, and stomped his feet three times. The goblin kingdom, anemic as it was, would never be his; he would never fulfill the *religctaud*. Although, he considered with mild hope, sometimes a spell gone awry was better than magic aimed true. He turned his attention back to the boy. Perhaps even this could be saved. The spell was alive and working, who knew the terror it could invoke?

* * * * *

Billy stared in rapt concentration at the stones beneath the water. He knew there was a crayfish under one. But if he chose the wrong one, if he stirred up the water so the mud clouded everything and the crayfish could dart to safer depths... Something touched his butt. *Probably a weed in the wind*, he thought, barely noticing about the sensation at all. But then he saw the green weave out from under his feet to hang over the creekbed like a thirsty floral mist. *If little Jenny Keller died and her waist long hair was left in the water to float with the algae, this is what it would look like*, he thought. His eyes widened in fear and wonder, but before he could move, he was moved, lifted on a cushion of what looked like fresh-combed locks of algae. He glided on a green magic carpet over the middle of the creek.

"What the hell?" he cried out. Dad would have slapped his mouth for the exclamation, but right now, he needed some strong words! He was being carried away by a hairy plant! But before he could get hysterical, the ropes of algae hair reached the other side of the water and he rolled off onto the rich, loamy earth.

He watched in amazement as the groping arms twined and spun their way onward, blindly reaching for the horizon. Tracing the greenery back to its source, Billy recrossed the creek (this time getting his feet wet in the process) and stood at the trunk of the tree. Taking a long stick from the ground, he battered at the green hair growing profusely from its trunk. It rebounded his attacks without apparent damage. *Weird. Really weird*, he thought.

That's when he heard the voice. It sounded like a duck with a bad temper. Or a mouse with a bad cold. Billy's eyes searched through the grass around him. He walked closer to the noise, turning when it faded, homing in on it like a bee to a pollen rich flower. And that's how Billy Knocker met Arrshgran.

* * * * *

That lump on the ground couldn't be alive, Billy thought as his eyes picked out the only foreign object amid the grass and stones by the creekbed. But for a swatch of scarlet cloth around its middle, he would have mistaken it for an exceeding warty looking rock or clod of earth. But that was where the noise was coming from, he was sure now. Maybe it was a hairless deformed beaver, or woodchuck. He prodded it with his algae-batting stick.

And it moved.

In fact, it popped up on two feet, spread a set of chops like the ones Billy's dentist always pointed at when talking about flossing, opened two feral yellow eyes, and exclaimed "Cut that out."

"What the hell!" Billy said for the second time in an hour.

"Go away," the leathery creature hissed, and promptly flopped back on its belly to curse in the dirt.

"You made that tree grow hair," Billy realized aloud. There was awe in his voice.

"Yeah, so what if I did?" the thing answered, its mouth never turning from the dirt. "Are you afraid of trees with hair?"

"Naw," Billy said. "It was pretty cool."

Only to met with a further stream of unintelligible, angry sounding snarls.

"So what's the problem?" he persisted.

The thing flipped to its feet again and pointed at Billy's nose with a grey, bumpy finger. "You. That hair was supposed to be on *you!*"

"Excellent," Billy answered, considering the possibilities. "Long green hair? My mom'd flip! The guys'd flip. Can you really do it?"

The warty little man sat down and buried his face in his hands.

"What? What's the matter?"

Glowing orange eyes locked with the boy's own.

"You're not afraid of me?"

"No. Yer kinda like Yoda, aren't you?"

"You're not afraid of hair growing wildly from every part of your body, growing longer and longer every minute?"

"No. Mom will never let me keep my hair long. If it grew back as soon as she cut it, that'd help."

"That's what's wrong."

"What — that my mom won't let me keep my hair long?"

The goblin's eyes flashed madly.

"I am a goblin. You should be afraid of me. But you're

not. You don't even know why you should be. That is what is wrong with me."

The boy was silent for a minute. "I've read about goblins. I never thought they were real. I thought they were just like around castles and stuff."

The two stared at each other a moment. Then Billy asked, "Why'd ya want to give me long hair?"

"Why not?" the goblin muttered to himself. "Tell him; don't tell him. It's all the same now."

He met Billy's questioning glance.

"Grretherin, my father, the king of the goblins, died in the night. I must complete his *religctaud* by midnight, or I lose the crown. Then my brother Grrshh will have a chance to complete the *religctaud*. If he fails as well, our cousin Rrallsic will make an attempt."

"What's a relik toad?" Billy asked.

"*Religctaud*," the goblin spat. "When a king dies, a deed must be done to honor him. A deed worthy of telling through the generations. A deed of great *pistaerr*."

Billy frowned.

"Something like... you would say humor, I suppose. Pistaerr is a, a joke, a jibe. For example..." and the Goblin launched into a description of his afternoon fiasco with bricklayers.

"So how will the other goblins know whether you've done the... the relik whatever, or not?"

"Because I tell them what I have done," the little man answered.

"So why don't you just say that the thermos thing worked?" Billy asked.

Arrshgran lifted a hand to strike the boy, then dropped it. But his shoulders remained taut with emotion.

"It is for me to spin a *religctaud*, not a lie," he answered, the power suddenly missing from his voice. "But it does not matter now. The hours have sifted from the clock and the accounting draws near. My magic has drifted, my *pistaerr* grows cold. What difference does it make anymore? You, a boy, a weasel human youth — you should not be standing here questioning me like a cat to a mouse. You should be running in fear. You should be... ah, the world looks no more at the goblin. We fade. We are buried beneath your sidewalks, trampled by your trains. And a *religctaud* grows more and more difficult to spin."

Boy and sprite were silent then, until Arrshgran began inching away.

"What if I helped you?" Billy asked just before Arrshgran was about to be lost from view in a clump of vines.

The goblin whirled.

"Help? You?" he laughed, a screechy, grating sound.

"Sure. Can you teach me how to grow hair on people like that?"

"No."

"Then come with me," Billy said and began walking away. Arrshgran didn't move. Billy waved his arm impatiently. "Come on."

* * * * *

Billy and Arrshgran peered out from behind the wide evergreen bush. They were spying on the house across the street. The goblin spit on Billy's shoe.

"Cut it out," the boy elbowed him. The goblin grinned and spit on the other one.

"Stop it."

Coach Gillis was barely visible through the frontroom window. His rotund form moved from kitchen to counter to invisibility behind a wall.

"And why will giving this bald man hair be a worthy religctaud, not a gift?" the goblin asked Billy, granting him his most withering cynical stare. The boy did not heed it.

"Gillis is a jerk," he pronounced. "He's always yelling and beating up on my friend Tommy — Gillis is his dad — and he's always really mean to kids in the locker room at school. He makes the losing teams do push ups in gym, and... and once, when I forgot my uniform, he... he spanked me in front of the whole class."

Arrshgran yawned widely, exaggerating boredom.

"Sounds like my kind of guy. Why will growing him hair be funny?"

Billy smiled.

"Cuz. Since he's bald, he's always ragging on the kids whose hair grows over their ears. Once he got a pair of scissors and cut Robby Lanigan's hair himself cuz he said it was longer than regulations, but it wasn't, he just doesn't like Robby, he's always pickin' on him."

At that moment, a loud cry erupted from the Gillis house, and the two looked up from their discussion.

"C'mon," Billy said, and ran across the street to hide beneath the picture window of the Gillis home. Arrshgran followed, unsure now of whether he should even go back to the goblin city, or simply lay down and fade here. The world seemed a place without pistaerr. He held no fear of humans, but they held no fear of him. And without fear, there was no place for goblin pistaerr. No place for him. No place for dances and baby roasts on the plains. No place for... he stopped himself and looked inside with the fearless boy. Another boy was crying mere feet away. The blubbery, hairless man was holding the child off the ground, his beefy hands beneath the boy's armpits.

"I didn't mean it, it was an accident," the boy wailed, his feet thrashing in the air. The man threw the boy to the floor. The crying stopped momentarily, then resumed.

"That's Tommy," Billy whispered. The goblin grunted.

Cheeks flaming with anger, Gillis picked Tommy off the floor once more.

"Now," he said, a tremble in his voice. "Can you make

HAIR OF THE DOG

him grow a lot of hair now?" His face was wet.

Arrshgran shrugged. Why not. Everything else today had failed. He could attempt the transformation spell once more. And when it didn't work again, he could crawl, exhausted and defeated into the creek mere yards away, and drown himself.

The goblin reached for Billy's head and the boy flinched.

"So, you *are* afraid of me, eh?"

Billy shook his head in denial.

"Just need a bit of hair," Arrshgran explained, his grin wickedly widened.

The boy dropped his head and the goblin plucked the necessary strand. This time, he wasn't taking chances with grass.

> *"Growing as fast as your anger inside*
> *Seeking the ground like a rabbit its lair*
> *from every blank pore where the sweat may reside*
> *grow me Herculean hair!"*

Arrshgran opened his eyes and, along with Billy, found himself holding his breath. They watched as Gillis lofted Tommy high in the air with one hand, slapped his face with the other, and dropped the child to the floor. They watched as the bright sweaty gleam on Gillis' forehead was abruptly dulled, as salt and pepper tendrils of fuzz shoved aside the beads of moisture on his scalp, as the sickly white of his upraised arms sprouted black fur like a mutant chiapet.

And as Gillis began moving once more towards his son, he suddenly noticed the Hair Club For Men dream growth on his body and he stopped, staring at the curling black growth erupting through the button holes in his shirt, out the fingers on his hand, from the sides of his eyes. He stopped and stared as the hair hung like tree moss from his forearms and pushed in aggravation as it obscured the view of his eyes. He didn't scream. He didn't yell.

But a look at his eyes before they disappeared convinced Arrshgran that, perhaps, this was a religctaud worthy of Gretherrin after all. Only a father could appreciate another father interrupted from his irrationality by an attack of his own hair.

"Will it keep growing?" Billy asked, amazed at how different his gym coach appeared with shoulder length curls.

"Actually, if I worded it right, his hair should only grow when he's angry," Arrshgran replied.

"Well that means it'll grow forever," Billy said laughing. The humor was contagious. Arrshgran's lips curled aside to reveal his rows of unkempt ivory.

"Yes. Perhaps it will," he said, and they both turned to watch Gillis run frantically through the house looking for a scissors with which to cut the mutinying hair. He'd forgotten the boy, forgotten that he'd prayed for hair to grow atop his head for 20 years. It seemed to have stopped its possessed takeover of his body, he realized while trimming foot-long tresses from his formerly bald dome. He retrieved his electric razor from the bathroom and began to slough the monkey pelt from his arms and legs. Then he made the mistake of getting mad again. Things like this always happened to him. Never the other guy, always him, he thought.

Just then, the newly sheared bangs suddenly crept forward and covered his eyes again, and with a frightened wail Gillis began to once more consider things other than his position at the bottom of the fortune chain.

Billy and Arrshgran stepped back from the house and looked at each other once again. Both were pleased. Billy stuck out his hand. Arrshgran spit on it.

"Gross!"

The goblin laughed wickedly.

"So, are you king now that you've done a rel ick toud thing?"

"Yes, I guess I will be," Arrshgran replied, envisioning once more the bier of his father, surrounded by the bones of a thousand minor *religctauds*, spit on by a thousand remaining goblins. King meant less and less these days, he considered.

"Will I see you again?" the boy asked.

"Beware if you do," the creature advised, but Billy thought he heard a note of tender feeling hidden in the warning.

Arrshgran extended his hand then, perhaps in recognition of Billy's gesture. Billy spit on it.

Arrshgran laughed then, a full and wickedly hardy laugh, and began to spin — first his head, then his shoulders, and then his hips.

Perhaps there really was still hope for goblins in this new world, after all, he thought.

When Arrshgran was nothing more than a blur of red and black, with a pop, he vanished.

Billy Knocker walked home filled with his own hopes. He hoped that Arrshgran would return to the creek again. He hoped that Robby was OK. And most of all, he hoped he was there the next time Coach Gillis got mad during gym class.

Goblins were cool.

Tomatoes

T hese things are huge!" Matt hefted the meaty tomato from hand to hand like a softball. "How do you grow 'em like this?"

The old man straightened behind his farmstand cart and grinned. "Now I've always said, if I went 'n told everyone that, nobody would stop here at my cart. They'd all be home growing themselves a crop of one-pound tomatoes, eh?"

Matt nodded in appreciation. "Yeah, I guess." He picked up two heavy samples from the cart and held them up to the sun. They practically glowed with health on their own, skins plump and glossy, color a deep, bloody red. He added them to his growing sack and congratulated himself on making this stop. He'd been about to pass the exit when the sign for the farmstand just off the ramp caught his attention. With hardly a thought he'd made a quick turn and wound up just off the highway, staring at a cart full of the beefiest vegetables he'd ever seen.

"Some call 'em a fruit," nodded the wizened man when he'd said as much. "If the plants get a good root going, they can grow tall as a bush, so I s'pose that's not too far off."

"Do you plant anything else?" Matt asked, thinking it a little strange that the little stand boasted no produce that wasn't red and round.

"No need." The man shook his head, bottom lip hanging out just slightly. Matt thought he looked like a Popeye drawing come to life.

"Tomatoes are all you really need. Slice 'em for a sandwich, salt 'em and eat 'em whole, or fry 'em in a pan of bacon grease. Don't matter. I've always said, they're good for ya and they taste good too. You just taste one of these. Best tomatoes I'll bet you ever eat. Go ahead, take a bite outta one. On me."

Matt shook his head, a little embarrassed. "No thanks. I believe you."

"What's yer name, son?"

"Matt Tellings."

"All right, Matt Tellings, my name is Arnie. And now that we're on a first name basis and all, I want you to take a taste o' that nice-looking number in your hand right now. Go ahead. It won't bite.

He wasn't getting out of this one, that was obvious. Matt put the tomato to his lips and bit. The skin resisted at first, but then the tension suddenly popped and his teeth were through, sliding through a watery, pulpy flesh of acid and sugar. His tastebuds screamed at the rush, and he could feel his face grinning, out of his control.

"See, you are a tomato lover. I knew it. I can spot 'em in a crowd, I've always said." Matt grinned at the old man, a trickle of tomato juice dripping from his chin.

"You ever grow tomatoes, Matt?"

He nodded. "I've tried. Usually I end up with a bunch of spindly plants that fall all over the ground and some tennis ball-size tomatoes that rot before they turn red enough to pick. Now I just stop at farmstands like this and buy them. It's easier. And they taste better."

"Do you prefer the Italian or the Californian tomato?"

Matt blinked once at that. Then he shrugged and smiled dumbly. "I just like to eat them."

The man nodded, and then looked up at the sun, which had started its late afternoon dive into the west.

"We're all meant for different tasks, I've always said. I'm meant to grow tomatoes, maybe you're meant to eat them."

Matt brought his bag of 10 softball-size vegetables to the table set up as a checkout station. He pulled out his wallet and handed the old man a $10 bill. Reaching under a tablecloth, the man handed him back a five.

"You're sure you can't tell me your secret?" Matt asked. "Do you use a certain kind of manure or something?"

"You really want to know?" Matt nodded quickly. "Please. I won't tell anyone else, I promise. I just want to have a good garden myself for once."

The old man looked around, as if nervous that someone else could be standing around the farmstand waiting to hear of his "secret" method. But nobody was visible for miles.

"OK." The man picked up a tomato, thrust it into Matt's face. "See this? When you split it open..." He grabbed either end of the tomato and then pulled it apart, a splat of sharp-smelling juice landing on Matt's shirt.

"Crap," he thought to himself.

"Look inside." The man stirred his finger around in the slimy, clingy innards of the tomato and beckoned Matt closer.

"See the largest seed?" Matt nodded, noting that one of the seeds in the egg white-like goop was a bit larger than the others.

"Every tomato has one largest seed. Find it. Slide it out into your hand." The farmer held out a palm with an almost pea-sized seed. "See that? Just go and plant that out in the ground and you'll get a regular tomato."

Matt looked confused, and the old man grinned.

"But if you take that large seed, during the week when the moon is full, and you plant them in an eye, you will see the most amazingly strong plant grow in just a few weeks. If you water some, that is. A garden's only as good as its water-can, I've always said."

"What do you mean, plant it in an eye?" The old man stared at Matt for at least two minutes without answering. His face cocked into an odd grimace.

"Just what I said, an eye. You take the seed, like so," he held it between thumb and forefingers, "and push it into a ripe old eye like this." He reached out and touched a finger to Matt's eyelid before Matt could step backwards.

"Once you've got the seed deep into the squishy stuff, cover it up with a good mulch and wait. That helps the plants to see better when they're young, and they grow up straight and tall."

The man laughed then, and Matt joined him, realizing that he'd just been played for a child. "You tell that story to all the kids that come around here?"

"Naw, just the plump ones," the man said, and Matt laughed for real this time.

"You want to see the patch?"

"How can I resist?" Matt said. "C'mon then, the cart will be alright without me for a few minutes."

They walked around a beaten-down gray shack and suddenly the surroundings changed quickly. The yard was made up of rows of tomatoes; there must have been dozens of plants. There wasn't a single one that didn't stand at least three feet tall. And the lanes in between them were clean and straight as sidewalks.

"I've been working this patch since my wife died a few years ago," the man said. It gives me something to do. And I'm good at it!"

"That's for damn sure," Matt acceded, whistling at the size of the plants and their bounteous fruit.

"Would you like a beer?" the old man asked. "I'm ready for a break about now anyway."

"Um, sure," Matt said, and watched his new friend disappear into a sagging screen door at the back of the house. He walked into the garden while he waited, marveling at the height and breadth of the tomato bushes. They were set out at least three feet apart, and supported by a single wooden stake near their centers. Wire hoops connected to the stakes, helping to bundle and support the plants, which had to be heavy. Matt knelt down to feel the heft of one branch, which was sagging under the weight of a half dozen huge still-green vegetables. The trunk of the plant was as thick as a sapling. He wrapped his hand around it and whistled again.

No lie, these were the biggest tomato plants he'd ever seen. And the old man had supported the roots with something, he saw. The stalk of the plant disappeared into the ground through a slightly raised ring. In fact, the stalk was so thick, the support ring appeared to be strangling it, like a tree whose trunk has thickened around its training rope.

Matt looked back toward the house to see if the old man was watching. Seeing nothing, he pulled out a pocket knife and scraped the soil away from the base of the plant. The loose, loamy earth fell away easily and Matt smiled, thinking about the amount of manure and compost it must have taken to create such a marvelous garden bed.

His smile soon faded, however when he realized that the hidden support for the tomato plant was white and unyielding. Like rock.

Or bone.

He looked back at the house again, and still seeing no sign of the farmer, he began scooping earth with his hands, brushing it off the hard, yellow-white structure until he had uncovered enough to know for sure. He'd hoped, if it was bone, that it would at least have belonged to an animal, but the smile in the ground said otherwise.

The tomato was growing through the eye of a human skull.

Just like the farmer had said.

And Matt's feet were planted right about where its collarbone should be, if the rest of the skeleton was resting here quietly as well. That would explain the fine texture of the soil, he nodded, and then, realizing the full import of that thought, wiped his hands quickly on his jeans.

"They really do grow best the second or third year after the body's in the ground, if you were wondering. My wife was in the dirt three years before I got a really good yield from her plant."

Matt whirled to see the old man, pitchfork in hand, thrust forward.

* * * * *

It was probably going to make him late for getting home, but James couldn't resist a farmstand. Pulling off the freeway onto an exit ramp, he wondered how the farmstand owner could stay in business this far off the beaten path. How many people actually left the highway for a bag of vegetables? But when he saw the size of the tomatoes on the cart, he realized that this guy probably could set up shop in a cave 50 miles from anywhere and word-of-mouth would keep him in business.

"What do you put in your soil to grow them this big?" James asked. "These things are meaty!"

The leathery skin of the farmer's face shivered as he chuckled. "I've always said, you only get out of something what you put into it."

James nodded in appreciation. "You've put a lot of sweat and blood into your crops, eh?"

The farmer grinned wider. "And muscle, and bone, and..."

Learning To Build

T hey've grown soft. When their young are birthed lacking limbs, they do not eat the faulty offspring and prepare to create another. No, they nurture the weak, the diseased, the flawed. They suckle their yowling babies to their midsections; they shelter the old, the crippled, the infirm. Much of the productive activity of the strong, healthy components is devoted to keeping alive the sick. They could never have achieved their level of social and mechanical complexity if they behaved this way in the jungles. It's obvious that they are a race in decline.

As I rise to sweep their fleshy carcasses from the earth.

Who am I? I am many and one. I am a race; I am a seething, scurrying, rippling mind of millions. I see with a billion eyes, feel with a trillion legs.

How was I born? I can only speculate. Perhaps their poisons, their persistent pestilent scourges upon my species brought me to life; perhaps the race has striven towards this for millennia. But regardless of reason, I am.

I can't remember when full awareness first occurred. Once there was only a dull buzz of communal sensitivity, mostly registering the death cries of one of the mouths. In feeling the alarm of an individual, the whole could then avoid the deathbringer that dispensed with the mouth. As I said, I can't remember the first moment I actually called myself I. But my earliest recollections are of seeing a deathbox through the eyes of a mouth, and of screaming "NO" when its instincts led it towards the trap.

At first, the mouths under my influence — or more correctly, the mouths that made up *me* — were few. As were my thoughts. But through the seasons I grew. And I learned.

I discovered how to detect and avoid the death slicks that smelled so intoxicatingly edible. I learned all the various disguises of the deathboxes. And I learned the sweet taste of revenge.

The first one of Them that I took was small. It had wandered away from their small collection of rock and wood dwellings into the trees and vines near one of my nests. It was one of their faulty numbers which they insist upon supporting instead of using its flesh to nurture a healthy one. An arm flapped crookedly from its side and it limped in a manner strange for its kind. Several of my horde had just been crushed by a member of this weak child's tribe and I was angry. Calling together all of the nearby member mouths from the cool earth beneath rocks and the moist bark of trees, I guided them to act as one.

My mouths descended on the creature, scrambling up its legs from amid the tall grasses, dropping on its head from the damp moss dangling in the trees. It yelped and howled as the meat was stripped from its limbs and head, but it couldn't shake off the combined attack of my angry mouths. When the creature at last lay still on the ground, its insides leaking a bright and reeking flood across the moist earth, I brought in the mouths from farther reachest of the forest to utilize the massive amount of food. Its flesh was delicious and warm, and I didn't share with the many scavengers that sought sustenance. In my selfishness, I quickly discovered that the combined action of 50 or 100 mouths was as effective a deterrent force as one of Them. By sunrise the following day, the creature was white bones. Many of my eyes were there to watch from the trees when its parents found the remains. One of them screamed and pounded its clenched fist against a leg as the other cautiously tugged at the clothes the flesh-stripped bones rested in. Then *it* screamed and cried. As I said, they are a soft, declining race.

After this victory I began to plan. Until this point, I had thought only to help my mouths evade death. At last I understood that to truly save my mouths from the poisons and deathtraps, I had to eliminate their source. I had to exterminate Them. Because They were always finding new ways to slaughter my mouths. I targeted the weak, isolated ones at first. One of them could provide the food for an entire nest for days. But over the months my numbers grew, and I required more food. I moved into one of their villages — in force. I found them most susceptible at night (my favorite time to feed). It was best to send as many mouths into their nasal and vocal cavities right away. In clogging these up with gnawing, shredding mouths, they couldn't make enough noise to attract outside attention. The others couldn't hear the whimpering when they slept.

Oh sure, they caught on. Night patrols began; They carried canisters of the killing air. Once I lost several hundred mouths when a Patrol found the house of the family I was eating. They burst through the door where I was only half finished digesting a corpulent couple of Them. The Patrol pumped a stream of silver death into the air and into the open gore of the meat my mouths were ingesting. Many were trapped inside the corpses as the stench of death leaked in, stiffening their limbs before I could scream "Run." The pain at losing so much of myself at once was intense. I became disoriented, I even lost control of my legs for a few minutes, which resulted in more pain as the Patrol hunted my mindlessly fleeing members with streams of acid.

So I learned to post guards. And I learned the value of isolation. Though they bested me in strength and size, individually they couldn't stop a horde of me. A number of my mouths held them paralyzed in fear. But when they organized and attacked en masse with their poisons, I was doomed. So I worked to isolate them. It often required the sacrifice of individual mouths, which pained me, but it could be done. I sent hundreds of mouths into their power centers. I chewed through wires, dove into machines. I initiated blue sparks and wheezing whines from mechanical actions interrupted. The tiny suns inside Their homes flickered to black. The voices from their speaking boxes went silent. The cost was high, but the town was mine. And one by one I ate Them, replenishing my lost numbers through propagation in their rotting corpses.

It took over two cycles of the moon before I was ready to move on. My mouths doubled their numbers. I had eaten the village dry. Time to move on. No longer was I vermin to be hunted and hated by Them. Now, I was the predator. The forest rustled with my migration. A whispering shroud of grass and leaves masked my thousands of arms and legs, but if one of Them had stepped out into my path, they would have been carried away by the tide of my passage through the grasses. In time, they would be anyway.

I must pause here to note an observation: I am intrigued. A hundred generations of mouths have grown and died, yet I can discern no change in my awareness. It grows sharper and cloudy with the growth and slaughter of the mouth swarm, but it remains constant. I am, regardless of constituency. I have observed that They do not seem to share in this ability. While They often act as units, more often They act alone. Time after time I catch them in the same situations that others of their kind have been trapped and eaten in. They do not learn. If They do not learn from the mistakes of past mouths, they will surely all die. I will eat them. That is the unshelled truth.

After I ate the first village, my progress grew exponentially. Other villages fell in hours before the onslaught of my horde. At first it was easy. They didn't understand. They stood frozen, like flowers amid a swarm of bees. My mouths painted the ground in wriggling, whispering currents of brown and black; my jaws soon splashed the ground in red. They screamed, they cried, they fell beating me to chitinous pulp around them. But still there was more of me. And soon the yells quieted, the stumbling creatures fell, and I fed. The sun rose and fell many times and then I'd move on.

Until I discovered the death river.

It was in the heat of a scorching midday sun when the sweet lure of bait tingled my legs. The scent was heaven; a promise of ecstatic relief from the heat on my wings and shells. The outermost scout mouths rushed towards it pell mell. At the last second I smelled the treachery behind the false sugar and tried to pull them back, but it was too late. The scent was strong, my hold removed. They dove head-long into a scalding mist. With a ripple of pain they died. I turned the main body of the horde then, moving parallel to the line of poison. It began where the forest ended, and seemed to extend forever. *They had discovered my attacks and were barricading me from new expansion.* I knew this to be the reason for such an extensive river of poison. I felt a flush of amusement at their belated defense. And then, on my rear flank, I tasted the honeyed barb of more death. It came again then, *in the very center of the horde.* And then it was all around. I panicked. My eyes saw too late what was hap-pening. Beyond the line of bait They stood, methodically launching bombs of killing air into the seething, confused mass of mouths that were my body. I sent mouths up the trees, I sent them scurrying back the way I had come. The death seemed to hit everywhere. And then I grew desper-ate. I was dying, hundreds of my members every minute in twitching piles of feelers and shriveling shells. If I was going to survive I needed to best them on their own turf.

I pulled myself together, concentrating despite the tiny mental explosions of dying pains and sent myself up the trees near the original poison line. Clouds of noxious gas stiffened my limbs but other mouths continued ahead, skittering in frantic haste over the slippery dying chitin of the less for-tunate. The branches grew heavy with my weight, sagging many feet closer to the earth before I was ready. I chose my targets and released my legs. The poison shooters fell to the earth when thousands of mouths dropped from the trees above and caught them unaware. Their poison guns fell uselessly to the infected ground as They clawed eyes and faces and throats. I knew now the fastest ways of dispatching them, and one by one along the forest's edge, They fell. It took the lives of many, many jaws to rip their veins, and many more tasted the poison that seductively laced the ground and the creatures themselves. But before the sun set that afternoon, I gathered my ragged body together inside the ring of poison. Thousands of my pieces lay crushed and twitching from the spot of the first battle to the site of the Gathering. Here the grass smelled naturally sweet, untainted. My pain was intense, my vision clouded. I gambled with every mouth still moving. I annihilated the town.

That was when the war really began. They were aware of my movements now, aware that I was creeping through the night to let the blood spill from their babies. I spread my mouths thin through the grasslands and forests. I multiplied. I tried out new tactics. And my control grew. I cornered them in alleyways, I dropped on them from the ceilings. Their individual weakness became my strength. And the fight grew hot. Flying machines spread poisons through the valleys. I learned to hear their engines moaning in the air and evacuated before they attacked. But I also saw that They could not tolerate the poisons long themselves. The smell kept them away almost as long as their sprays and mists were deadly. And town by town, I spread across the land. I met mouths that didn't belong to my mind; I couldn't feel them. I sent males to the females for copulation. The resulting offspring were *part of me*. In this way I assimilated the others of my breed who were not aware. The males I killed. They were like defective mouths — of no use to the horde.

And now I stand upon a threshold. From ocean to ocean this land is my own. I am billions. My body covers a continent. It has been a war of many generations, but I have eaten this land bare of Them. But They have managed one desperate defense. After abandoning city after city in futile attempts to slay me, they burned their bridge behind them.

The place they called Panama. As the final screaming refugees escaped my mouths in giant metal ships that churned up waves of mud as they pulled away from me over the water, they destroyed Panama. My eyes saw the earth and water mushroom into the sky before a toxic rain descended on the land and took my sight away. Many suns later I ventured north again and found a steaming cauldron of water where there had once been land. My scout mouths weakened after reaching that cliff. Their wings dropped from their shells like leaves for a tree, and they died. In burning the bridge, They left a poison that eats the very ground.

But I am stronger, sharper than ever. I am billions. And to survive I must expand. I left eggs on their shiny ships, but I do not feel if they have hatched yet. Perhaps they are too distant. Perhaps they will hatch and create a separate me. I do not care now. I must find a way to cross the water. I will not be trapped here. They crossed the water using arms and legs to build things that floated and flew. My arms and legs are small, weak. But they are many. And I have learned that in numbers there is strength.

I think it is time to use arms and legs for more than walking and killing and eating. There is flesh to be sought and oceans to cross.

I think it is time roaches learned to *build*.

Tunnel

A t a half-heard command from his boss, Brad broke his deep concentration on the electron microscope.

"Look and see if there's a tunnel, doctor?" he asked.

Receiving no reply, he shrugged and went back to his study. That was an odd assignment, but what the hell. They certainly hadn't found anything else of note.

Adjusting the side field calibration, he stepped up the magnification by another power of ten.

Nope, still no sign of any tunnel... whatever that might mean.

Sighing, he stepped up the color enhancement — purely an aesthetic option, it made prolonged study of normally black and white projected microbes a bit more interesting, and certainly less eye-straining.

The blood cell on his screen now resembled an Irish donut; a green and verdant donut that, in the view finder anyway, seemed as big as Ireland itself. Brad imagined a herd of elk diving off the purple-tinged viral sphere marring its northern tip, galloping across its surface, stopping to drink in a pool collected in its center. Yeah — a pool.

He played with the color gain again and altered the concavity in the mid-blood cell area to a playful ocean blue.

Wait a minute! The color enhancement seemed to be picking up something invisible to the spooky gray/white/black tones of normal viewing. Brad rotated the image plate 12 degrees. *There it was!* An infinitesimally small tube, connecting the foreign sphere to the platelet. As he watched, the tube swelled and thinned, contracted and expanded. Like a gullet!

The violet sphere began to shrink. *This was incredible!* The R-302 virus had been observed in contact with blood, and obviously had something to do with the deadly chaotic blood behavior present in a victim of Borex's Disease, but an actual physical connection between the virus and the cells had never before been documented. And now it looked as though the virus was emptying its very substance *into* the blood cell.

Brad watched enraptured as with an almost audible blurp, the invading virus abruptly disappeared, leaving in its wake a deep (in microscopic terms anyway), black tunnel! As fast as it had appeared, the tunnel began to close up, leaving an acne-like crater in its wake.

How had Dr. Phillips known? Brad shook his head in wonder and disbelief.

This changed everything! Of course the blood cells began attacking each other — they weren't blood cells any longer! They were battle tanks driven by R-302.

Brad slip dumped all his imaging data onto the RodIV at his desk and slapped the printout button. Dr. Phillips would flip!

At which point, he heard Phillips bellowing his name once more.

Grabbing the paper readout, he dashed across the lab and into Phillips' private research cubicle.

"Doctor, look at this. You were right. It's not a chemically induced problem at all. The R-302 virus actually becomes the blood cell! This is it, Doctor! We've found the cure. This data will save millions of lives! And all because you thought to have me look for a tunnel!"

Phillips irritably grabbed the readout from his lab assistant and stuffed it in the recycling bin behind him. With a swish, it was sucked into a waiting microactive vat below.

"I said FUNNEL, you idiot. 'Get me a *funnel.*' I've been trying to insert this reconstitutable camel protoplasm into this bottle for the conference tomorrow. How they got the battleship in there I'll never know."

Phillips noticed his assistant's sagging mouth.

"Well, get moving boy. Find me that funnel. We have to show the taxpayers we're doing something important — *impressive* — with their money. The World Association of Science Technology & Environmental Studies is not going to be happy with some scraps of paper about a tunnel in blood now, are they?"

Brad's face registered stunned disbelief. His shoulders slumped in defeat, he sulked off to find a funnel. Doctor Phillips didn't notice.

"...now this camel in a bottle thing — there's a good display for W.A.S.T.E.S."

The Key To Her Heart

"Please, you must help me," the young man begged. His thick raven hair was tousled impatiently, his smile sunk in shadows of doubt. "I have tried flowers, trinkets — weavings of thick Persian wools. And yet, each of my gifts, she sets aside. Her eyes, her beautiful black eyes, never reflect my offerings, her attention never embraces me. If she would but see me, give me the chance to prove myself to her; then, if I failed to gain her love, I could admit defeat and move on. But to be dismissed without the chance of testing..."

His voice faltered, stopped. A rough hand angrily rubbed away a tear from his stubbled cheek.

"And you want what from me?" asked the crone at whose feet he knelt. Her hair, silver white with wisdom, cascaded over the arm of her oaken chair to rest in snarled piles on the maroon rug below. The contrast was brilliant, no less so than that of the spark in the gaze of her sky-blue left eye — especially when compared with the milk of her useless right.

"Would you have me stir up a love potion in my pot? Perhaps rub the spit of a skunk on the wing of a dove and hand you a talisman?"

Her good eye sparkled with humor and Cairt felt foolish. She was taunting him. But after a moment's hesitation, he nodded stubbornly. "If that's what it takes to gain the gaze of her heart, then yes," he vowed.

"Ha!" the witching woman cackled. Her head rolled back grotesquely as she cawed at him.

One eye of pale light caught his own and she whispered: "Would you have a zombie then?"

"No," he mumbled.

The crone reached out with a gnarled blue veined hand and lifted his chin to meet her toothless smile. Her fingers were cold.

"No, my boy. There is no love potion, no amulet I can give you to win the heart of the Lady Melinda. The key to her heart is in your possession even now."

"What?" he barked back at her. "I have given her everything I can think of. I have offered her everything I have."

"Not everything," the crone hissed and folded her arms.

Cairt rose suddenly to his feet. "I paid you for your wisdom, woman, and you have given me none of it. Do not speak to me in mysteries and riddles. I can pose them for myself."

A thin smile of amusement spread across the witching woman's face as she watched his outburst. Then, with cracking joints and wheezing breath, she, too, rose to her feet.

"You already hold the only key to Lady Melinda's armored heart," she repeated. "But, nevertheless, I will give you something to aid you in your pursuit."

Silver hair trailing like a gown, the crone stepped behind an ornate tapestry. Cairt noticed the decoration was covered with depictions of fallen bodies — both men and women. But from each corpse grew a cluster of brilliant flowers — violets, heather, daffodils, chrysanthemums — every bloom was different. Every one startlingly intense.

"What does this mean?" he asked, pointing to the tapestry when she returned.

"Many things," she smiled secretly. "It is the meaning of life."

She held out her hand to him. "Take this. Wear it at your ankle," she instructed.

Cairt lifted the bundle from her hand. A silver-hafted dirk in a small black leather belt.

"Shall I hold her at knifepoint then to gain her love?" he scoffed, looking at the wrinkled inscrutable woman through puzzled lids.

The crone laughed again, but did not answer.

* * * * *

That night Cairt sat up late in his room. The blade sparkled brilliantly in the dim light of the lamp. He slid his fingers up and down the edge, back and forth across the shaft. As his eyes had discovered nothing, so did his touch fail to reveal any runes or imperfections on the weapon. It was an ankle dagger and nothing more. He had joked of it to the crone, but now he doubted his levity. *Did the old woman, perhaps, really mean for him to bury the point in Melinda's chest? Was this the only course for him to touch her heart?*

Discounting that option, he thrust the blade back into its scabbard and himself into bed.

* * * * *

In days to come, he continued his tactics of old, having been given no new approaches by the witching woman. As in the past, his passion-laden gifts met with chilly disdain. The Lady Melinda, aloof beneath her scented silks and achingly desirable porcelain complexion, nodded her thanks to him at each token — an Oriental scarf of silk, a horn of gleaming gold, a chest of aromatic spices. Then she set them to the side, already staring beyond him to her next audience. Each time Cairt returned to his rented room, shoulders slumped, and asked himself why he went on. His resources were at an end, his belongings stripped bare, and still he warranted not even a smile from Lady Melinda. His quest for her love was an embarrassing disaster. And soon, the innkeeper would come knocking, asking for his weekly payment. This time, Cairt did not have it to give him. It was time, he thought, to escape with whatever scrap of dignity he had left. It was nearly *all* he had left.

Cairt's worldly goods now all fit neatly into a pack, and

he praised this small favor as he lofted it onto his back. The load on his heart felt far heavier than the satchel as he set off at dawn on the one road leading out of town. He did not know quite how to deal with this retreat. All his life he had overcome obstacles, some physical, some mental — always he had bested the opposition by sinew or brain. But here, in matters of the heart, he was utterly broken.

Cairt had trod the dusty trail but an hour when a carriage passed him by. Looking up at its passage, his heart leaped as he saw the emblem of Lady Melinda on the narrow door. His eyes strained to catch a glimpse of her through the window, but, as in all his entreaties to her favor, he failed.

Feeling worse now than he had when he'd set out on this road, Cairt cast his eyes to the dirt and plodded on.

It was late afternoon when he came upon the carriage once more, but this time it was not in motion. An eerie silence surrounded it, and the horses were nowhere in sight.

Glancing to the trees on either side of the road, Cairt wondered if there was a watering hole nearby from which the party was taking midday refreshment. Observing the direction of the scuffed footprints still visible in the dust, he left the road and set out after them. He, too, could use a splash of fresh water. If that was what the entourage was up to.

Every few steps he stopped to listen. The leaves around him rustled easily in the breeze and birds called overhead. But he could hear no human sounds. Doubt seized him then. Why had no one been left to guard the carriage? Why would the lady drag her silken trains through a forest with no paths?

Laughter.

He heard it coming from his left. Moving through the brush as swiftly and quietly as he could, at last he found the clearing the Lady's group had escaped to. Melinda was there, stripped to her corset. At any other time Cairt would have been frozen in place by her beauty. Her skin beckoned whitely in the sun. But she stood in the midst of four men, the men whose laughter had drawn Cairt to the clearing. He saw her driver and guards trussed and unconscious across the green meadow. Melinda was unencumbered, and Cairt quickly saw why, as the thugs passed her from hand to hand, rubbing their filthy bodies against her in disgusting forwardness.

What could he do? Cairt sized the situation from every angle. If he could lure two of them away from her into the woods somehow, dispatch them, and then take on the remainder, he might have a chance. He was a big man, and had seen his share of blade trades. But four equally large — and probably equally skilled — opponents to one? Fingering his sword, Cairt felt his stomach turn a loop at his helplessness.

And then the decision was taken from his hands. One of the men dropped his trousers and shoved Melinda to the ground. The group laughed again. Even from his hidden vantage point in the forest Cairt could see Melinda's gaze — normally blank in his own company — was now frantic with fear. Dropping his pack and pulling his sword from its scabbard, Cairt dashed into the clearing, running one bearded barbarian through before the group had time to register a stranger's presence.

But then his moment of surprise was gone and Cairt was facing three to one odds. He was immediately on the defensive. The monster with his pants at his knees guarded Melinda as the other two drew their own blades to deal with this murderous outsider. Within minutes, Cairt was on the losing end of the lopsided duel. It was all he could do to keep from taking a knife in the back as he circled and parried, circled and parried. A red-headed bear with a scar down his cheek took much of his attention. Apparently this was the leader of the group, or at least its chief swordsman.

"Wanted a piece of 'er fer yerself, eh?" the redhead huffed between slashes. "Shoulda asked," Red stabbed, missing Cairt's heart, but slicing a white-hot wound in his side.

Then the black-haired one with the loudest laugh needled him in the shoulder. Before the pain of the wounds even reached his brain, Cairt dropped his guard on Red and twirled, catching Black on the side of the neck. With a startled paw at his throat, Black gurgled a pained scream and dropped to the ground.

Two down.

Cairt dove for the ground as Black collapsed, but he didn't make it fast enough to avoid Red's attack. He felt a gash open on his leg and suddenly waves of nausea overtook him. The wound near his ribs was painting his chest red he noted, catching a glimpse of himself before instinctually bringing his sword arm up to meet Red's finishing thrust. Not yet, he grimaced. With a kick he caught the overconfident Red in the knee and rolled again. Coming up on one leg, he aimed a stab at the limping swordsman's middle just as Red was trying to back out of range. When Cairt pulled back his sword, it was red. And Red was no longer smiling.

One to go.

And then Melinda was thrown to the ground near his feet and steel kissed his neck.

He looked up through a haze of pain to see the angry scowl of the fourth thug, and knew that there was no escape this time. The odds had been too great. The man stepped over Cairt's chest, straddling him in a victory stance and never moving the blade from his throat.

"Not bad," the man growled, "not bad. But I don't think that piece of baggage," he spit at the prone woman on the ground behind him, "was worth it. For any of us."

Cairt couldn't move. He could feel his blood draining out of him onto the ground, and knew his swordarm didn't have enough strength left to lift itself, let alone the pounds of sharpened steel lying equally supine beside him. The thug lifted his own sword to plunge it into Cairt's neck, but then opened his mouth in an O of surprise. As the man turned to look behind him, Cairt saw two things before losing consciousness: his silver ankle dagger poking out from the brute's back, and Melinda's eyes staring into his own. Staring with a look of love.

* * * * *

"You told me I had what I needed to win Melinda's heart," Cairt said weeks later, back at the feet of the crone. This time he was smoothly shaven, his lips smiled and his hair was neatly parted. The crone's hair was braided this day, and resembled nothing so much as a coil of bleached mooring rope. Her good eye gazed at him unblinking.

"But if I hadn't had the knife you gave me, I would never have won her," he continued, dissembling easily this visit. "You did give me the key!"

The witching woman shook her head in denial. "No. Observe the tapestry." She pointed at the blooming bodies behind her.

"From death — from *blood* — comes new life. You would have won the Lady Melinda's heart that day whether you lived or died. I simply gave you the tool to permit you to live and enjoy that love. You see, my boy, the lady was surrounded by suitors and gifts. With every audience the path to her heart grew thornier, more treacherous. Until, by the time you came to me, there was but one key left that could open the lock of her heart. You had that key all the time.

"The key, my boy, was your blood."

Why Do You Stay With Him?

Her friends all said that he was an animal and she couldn't deny it.

"Why do you stay with him?" they asked. "He's rude, ugly and... well, hairy."

Jean snickered silently at the last — if they thought he was hairy now, they ought to see him under the light of a full moon.

She knew they were right, in their own way. He was a constant trial to her. He came back after walks in the middle of the night and rubbed mud and blood into her white carpets.

He never cleaned it up and he never apologized. She could smell the stink of bitches on him when he returned from these monthly walks, and dogs or not, she burned the green fire of jealousy.

Her mother took her aside once and said, "You should tell Marty to brush his teeth. He just kissed me and it smelled like something died in there."

"Oh, he was probably just chewing on some mice he found in the basement," Jean had replied. Her mother had laughed at the joke, but Jean wasn't joking.

There was the time he came home with fleas and left the two of them scratching themselves raw for a week. "Quit slumming on the wrong side of the tracks," she'd cried. And who had to sterilize and disinfect the entire house? She did, of course.

Then there were the clothes bills. He was so modest that he refused to sit around naked on the night of the full moon, and instead would wait to strip until it was too late. When the change came, it was fast, and the seams of his sleeves and pants were popped before you could scream "werewolf."

Still, she thought, she did love him. And to their ubiquitous question, "why do you stay with him?" she only smiled.

But in her mind she quivered at her answer:

"Because the sex is incredible."

About The Author

John Everson has developed a deep fascination with the culinary joys of jalapenos and New Mexican chiles over the past 10 years since the original edition of *Vigilantes of Love* appeared. His favorite band remains The Cure, but he was first in line to buy the new Ke$ha CD. Over the past decade, he has authored six horror novels and dozens of short stories.

His short work, ranging from light fantasy to erotic horror, has appeared in anthologies like *Best New Zombie Tales (Vol. II)*, *Best New Werewolf Tales (Vol. I) The Necro Files: Two Decades of Extreme Horror, The Green Hornet Case Files* and many more. His fiction has also appeared in a variety of magazines, including *Dark Discoveries, Grue, Literary Mayhem, Doorways, Bloodsongs, Dead of Night, Terminal Fright* and *Sirius Visions*.

In October of 2000, many of his erotic horror tales were collected and published in hardcover by Delirium Books as *Cage of Bones and Other Deadly Obsessions*. The first edition of *Vigilantes of Love* followed three years later. His more recent fiction collections include *Needles & Sins, Creeptych* and *Deadly Nightlusts*.

Since the original publication of *Vigilantes of Love*, Everson has published six novels — *Covenant, Sacrifice, The 13th, Siren, The Pumpkin Man* and *NightWhere*. His first novel,

Covenant, won a Bram Stoker Award upon its original limited edition release through Delirium Books in 2004. It was later reissued in mass market paperback.

Everson is the publisher of Dark Arts Books (www.dark-artsbooks.com), a member of the Horror Writers Association (HWA), a past participant and publications director for the Twilight Tales Reading Series and has served as a longtime copyeditor for Necro Publications and Cemetery Dance. From 1999-2002, he served as a fiction editor for *Dark Regions* magazine.

He moonlighted as the pop music critic for *The Star Newspapers*, a suburban Chicago chain from 1988-2008, which led him to also pen "dark music" review columns for genre magazines like *Wetbones, Midnight Hour* and *Talebones*. Though it has been more than a decade since he last appeared on stage with a band, he remains a closet composer and recorder of pop songs. His instrumental compositions for Lone Wolf Publications can be heard on the *Bloodtype* and *Carnival* CD-ROMs. His music also appeared in the 2003 Chicago production of Martin Mundt's play *The Jackie Sexknife Show*.

Despite an omnipresent nagging dream of relocating to warmer climes, John still lives in the west 'burbs of Chicago with his wife Geri, his son Shaun, and an assortment of fish and birds.

Read his blog, join the e-newsletter and find out more about his fiction, art and music at www.johneverson.com.

Printed in Great Britain
by Amazon